second degree tampering

second degree tampering

writing by women

SYBYLLA FEMINIST PRESS
MELBOURNE 1992

Sybylla Co-operative Press and Publications Ltd.
3rd floor Ross House
247-251 Flinders Lane
Melbourne 3001
Australia

First published by Sybylla Feminist Press, 1992

Copyright © Sybylla Press, 1992

Copyright © to individual pieces remains with the author.
All Rights reserved. Without limiting the rights under copyright reserved above, no part of this publication may be reproduced, stored in or introduced into a retrieval system, or transmitted, in any form or by any means (electronic, mechanical, photocopying, recording or otherwise), without the prior written permission of both the copyright owner and the above publisher of this book.

Text and cover design by Lin Tobias
Lin Tobias Design and Illustration
rear 252 Brunswick Street
Fitzroy 3065
Australia

Typeset in Berkeley Oldstyle and Franklin Gothic by Mark Davis.

Printed by The Australian Print Group
Suite 7/653 Mountain Highway
Bayswater 3153
Australia

second degree tampering: writing by women

ISBN 0 908205 10 4

1. Australian literature - women authors. 2. Australian literature - 20th century. 3. Feminism - Literary collections.
I Sybylla Feminist Press.

The cover illustration shows a detail of 'Untitled' by Joan Letcher, reproduced with her kind permission. Joan Letcher is represented by Michael Wardell, 13 Verity Street Gallery.

contents

second degree tampering	SYBYLLA	vii
beautiful lotus forest	MAYLYN LAM	1
still waters run deep	NOELLE JANACZEWSKA	3
goin' 'ome	RUBY LANGFORD 'GINIBI'	7
i look at a star	SUSAN LAURA SULLIVAN	12
swooping firebird	MONICA RASZEWSKI	14
in edith's case	PHILIPPA MOYLAN	21
once i was fou roux's lover	MARION CAMPBELL	27
stationmaster	LINDA MARIE WALKER	30
in a shoebox packed with cotton wool	CHRISTINE EDWARDS	40
eight-eighty-89	DEBBIE WESTBURY	45
what a waste	GIG RYAN	47
typist	LAUREN WILLIAMS	51
safer than sex	LAUREN WILLIAMS	52
footplate classics	EVELYN	53
in search of princess panda	EVELYN	57
sister jessie	MARY BASTABLE	60
bloody marys	SARAH WATERSON	63
untitled	VICKI PINGLE	68
coping	VICKI PINGLE	69
outside it snows	JYANNI STEFFENSEN	70
the prowler	MARION CAMPBELL	82
the room	JORDIE ALBISTON	84

rape scene	JORDIE ALBISTON	86
compass and map	GIG RYAN	88
bye-bye barbie	ROSEMARY NISSEN	89
thirteen	DIANE FAHEY	90
arachne and the bogeyman	JAN MATTHEWS	91
a ghost in the kitchen	FRANCES STEPHANS	95
in the city	RAE LUCKIE	98
in the early afternoon	TRISH McNAMARA	103
pretty deadly tidda business	JACKIE HUGGINS	107
for the record	SARA HARDY	116
scabs	TERESA SAVAGE	120
fashion statement	LISA BELLEAR	124
women's liberation	LISA BELLEAR	126
package my spirit	LISA BELLEAR	128
the journey	LILLIAN PREDIC-YOKSICH	130
the houses of pleasure	ANNETTE BLONSKI	134
eins, zwei, drei	LINDA WESTE	140
continental drift	BRIGITTE BARTA	143
like a banshee wail	LUCY JEAN MROZIK	146
transfer fee	GIG RYAN	151
memoir	GIG RYAN	152
album	JOANNE BURNS	153
terminal	ANNA GIBBS	156
i, pronoun	JORDIE ALBISTON	166
as blind as a blue sky in australia	ANGELA SEWARD	168
from common knowledge	JAN McKEMMISH	174
notes and acknowledgements		180

second degree tampering

TOWARDS A POLITICS OF IDENTITY

second degree tampering tells many stories. Personal and collective identities - refigured as active, problematic, sometimes enabling, always uncontainable - are the common concerns of this writing. The pieces collected here complement and resonate with each other to produce a text of complexity and possibility. For readers, this writing by thirty-seven women offers challenge and promise.

In many ways *second degree tampering* is a text of and for the nineties. It is created from a contemporary feminist politics which recognises and seeks out differences; not in an attempt to manufacture some infinite diversity between women, but in order to counteract the homogenising and exclusionary practices of modern society. We are interested in creating and maintaining a particular cultural space; one in which questions of importance to feminists can continue to be investigated, and the validity of writing by and for women is affirmed.

Women's struggles and feminist movements are far from over and remain predicated on the transformation of women's lives. However, developments both within and distinct from feminism make it impossible now to speak simply of women as if a shared identity bonds 'us' all. Feminist politics have necessarily become more complex, as have the concepts of women and gender, as the various feminisms address issues such as race, ethnicity, class, age, sexuality, employment, motherhood.

Acknowledging and exploring the differences between women focuses attention on the historical, social and cultural contexts in which all identifications take place. The writing in this collection reminds us of these material conditions which produce particular identities, and which are not only open to description and analysis, but also to challenge and transformation. This recognition of the historical production of our differences does not, however, render the category of 'woman' redundant. It remains the point of departure for any feminist politics, transforming 'identity' into a site within which the act of identifying as a woman and with other women can then function as a strategic political act.

second degree tampering is not interested in searching for an authentic or universal 'female identity'. After all, we are not made into who we are simply by our experiences of life and the choices we make. Our identities are largely dependent on the cultural meanings which position women. The writing in this collection is interested in these cultural processes by which we make sense of our selves and our worlds. The focus is on new ways of writing and thinking about women, ways which understand the very slipperiness of identity, asking not so much 'who are we' as 'how and why do we question who we are' and 'who do we want to be?' This text explores the ways identities are discovered, experienced, articulated and redefined; it is motivated not simply by the wish to understand women's lives and experiences, but by the feminist desire to change them.

WOMEN WRITING

Writing has always been important to feminism, serving to inspire and motivate women by representing new possibilities and producing new understandings, drawing women together and seeming to cut across social divisions. Crucially, writing is a site within which women can come to understand the ways in which language not only shapes and colours but ultimately constitutes our experience of the world as gendered subjects.

Much of the recent women's writing in Australia is notable for its concern with aspects of identity. But we would want to question the degree to which this writing is politically radical, and the degree to which realist writing about female experience can resist its too easy co-option by the familiarising therapeutic processes of the bourgeois press. We would also want to remember that the ways in which writing is practised and understood within feminism can themselves carry exclusionary assumptions: a shared language and literacy; a common understanding of what makes 'good' writing; a privileging of written over oral traditions.

In putting this collection together, we looked for writing which does one or both of two things. Firstly, writing which is aware, be it at the unconscious or the conscious level, of the conditions of our constitution as particular kinds of identities, writing which stops us from forgetting how it was that we were made into who we are. Secondly, writing which, having reached this understanding of the fictionality of our lives, starts to tell other stories and to use language differently.

BEING A FEMINIST PRESS

second degree tampering continues Sybylla's commitment to publishing and writing which radically challenges hegemonic ideas about writing and women. However, Sybylla's role as a feminist press has changed dramatically in the past three years.

Founded as a printery in 1976 and commencing its innovative publishing programme in 1982, Sybylla set out to challenge the hierarchical and misogynist organisation of commercial printing and publishing work, with collective decision making and work practices that gave new and feminist-socialist meaning to the lived politics of labour.

Like other small independent and politically committed presses, Sybylla is currently struggling to stay afloat. The printing presses were relinquished in late 1988 to offset publishing debts. Sybylla continues as a collective of unpaid workers, our publishing projects reliant on fundraising activities and occasional grants.

Our role as feminist publishers has become more problematic. The discovery of the 'women's market', the construction of 'women's writing' as a genre and 'women's studies' as a discipline, have ensured an increased representation of women writers within 'mainstream' commercial publishing. Yet despite women's increased visibility within the writing scene, it is clear that their inclusion is a conditional and selective one. Writers who attract attention, writers whose books are proven sellers, writers whose work can seemingly be assimilated into broader trends or into the profitable niche of 'women's writing' for the generic woman reader; these women may be published by 'mainstream' publishers. Without denying the potential of this writing to disturb or challenge the demands of the commercial market, access to writing which is explicitly radical or experimental continues to be reliant, in the main, on small alternative presses.

Simply publishing writing by women is not enough. Contemporary feminist politics and historical circumstances require more subtle and complex interventions. We understand our role as feminist publishers to be the renegotiation of the terms and relations of cultural production as they position women.

The production of *second degree tampering* by Sybylla is an assertion of the continued importance of publishing women's writing from an avowedly feminist position, with a willful disrespect for the values of commercial publishing.

THE COLLECTION

The starting point for this collection was a recognition that the ways of representing individual and collective identities are limited by the interpretative stories of 'our' culture. We were interested to collect writing which challenges or revises the dominant and familiar versions of personal, cultural and national identity.

Sybylla began work on this collection in September 1990, publicising the project and requesting submissions through book clubs, regional writing groups, educational institutions, literary magazines and community radio. The editorial process involved us in reading more than three hundred and fifty manuscripts, gradually narrowing down our selection until the final shape of the collection emerged.

Our readings of manuscripts were not shaped in isolation, but with re-reading, discussion and the insights gained by considering each piece alongside others. Individually and as a collective, we selected pieces which spoke to us and in some way met with our beliefs about the politics of women's writing. Selection was often difficult as each of us responded to, enthused over, and advocated for those pieces we thought should be included. Our discussions continually returned to questions about the exploration of identity, the politics of feminism, and the self-consciousness of writing.

Apart from selecting manuscripts, our role has included working with writers and editing individual pieces; shaping the collection through ordering of texts; framing them for the reader through their physical presentation as a book, the look of the page, the design of the cover, the choice of title. In making these editorial decisions we have tried to indicate particular readings for the text, but not determine a singular one.

second degree tampering was made possible by women working together from a shared commitment to feminist politics and an understanding that our collective process would strengthen rather than diminish the text. This is a collection which is more than the sum of its constituent parts.

'AUSTRALIAN' WRITING

This collection contains the work of 'Australian' women writers; a decision that reflects the history of Sybylla as a response to the material conditions of publishing in this country. In its fifteen years, Sybylla has maintained a commitment to radical cultural debate in Australia, and to making available writing by women which would otherwise remain unpublished.

The increasing domination of the Australian publishing scene by multi-national companies and books by non-Australian - predominantly English and North American - writers, makes this task even more pressing.

This is not to say, however, that we subscribe to simple notions of a 'national culture', much less to 'nationalist literature'. Instead, we are interested in cultural interventions which lay bare the exclusions assumed by an 'Australian identity'; in writing which recognises Australia as colonised and colonising, and addresses the presence of indigenous peoples and the vast population of immigrants who are not of Anglo-Saxon backgrounds.

We are interested in the intersections between the categories of 'Australian' and of 'Woman', and in the questions of representation and cultural difference that cut across them both.

Notions of identity are often determined by concepts of place, yet life in Australia is experienced by many women through dispossession or displacement. In *second degree tampering* many women have written of journeys to, from and within this place called Australia. Journeys of discovery, imaginary travels, forced movements, escapes. The 'statelessness' of women, whether oppressive or liberating, is a recurrent motif throughout this collection.

Australia's history is one of invasion and colonisation, its nationalist myths those of men and manhood, its dominant voice one of self-conscious individualism. The peculiarly masculinist cast of dominant narratives of Australian character and cultural history pose particular challenges to Australian women writers and feminist cultural politics in this country.

READINGS

In *second degree tampering,* by putting one piece here and another there, we have tried to suggest ways of reading even though there can be no one simple reading of any text. We had no wish, however, to provide a guided tour through the collection, and there are no neat starting points or conclusions. The works, independently of each other and as a collection, will inevitably mean different things to different readers. The writers too will become readers of their own fictions, now subtly transformed by their proximity to other writings and by the materiality of the book.

Readers will need to make their own sense of this text. Many of the pieces resist familiar reading strategies of identification and narrative expectation, thereby forcing readers to an awareness of their complicity in producing meanings. While identification can be a strong and moving way of reading texts, this collection reminds us that it is not the only way and that it can sometimes lead readers into traps, dead-ends, or compromising situations. We have attempted to promote different reading strategies so as to create alternatives for women's readings of themselves and their worlds.

We hope that each reader's encounter with *second degree tampering* affirms the validity of a politics which identifies women as its subject, a complex subject, and the writing and reading of female experience as transformative political acts. We also hope this text will generate different and radical ways of thinking about women, writing and identity, and enable readers to explore new ways, both personal and collective, of seeing, telling, living.

beautiful lotus forest

MY NAME IS MAYLYN LAM. The name is a hybrid, as I am, of Chinese and European origins. Maylyn is an anglicised remaking of Mei Ling, the pinyin version of a name that I could not recognise in chinese characters nor utter with the musical intonation that gives Chinese words their meaning. I can write my surname though. This is a pictogram of two trees, and means 'forest'. Lam is not a common surname in Asia, if it is a name at all. Saying it to Chinese people overseas, I have often been informed that it is probably really Lim. My father pronounced it more like Lum.

My name is Maylyn Lam. In Chinese languages, the surname precedes the first name. The Mei of Mei Ling means 'beautiful', the Ling means 'lotus'. I have an older sister Sulyn who is a delicate lotus. I have a younger sister whose middle name is Lylyn, pretty lotus. Her first name is Maria. Collectively, these names make us a forest of lotus flowers.

'Number one daughter, number two daughter, number three daughter,' my father would pronounce proudly, lining us up in descending order like notes on a piano scale. 'Number one son' was named, surprisingly, Peter. 'Peter the rock' my mother, a lapsed Catholic and a lapsed Italian, would say. Indeed, in the folklore of the family, Peter turned out to be very stubborn. Life is hard for number one sons. David, after him, was less frequently referred to as number two son. This was a more ignominious position in a filial system than any daughter need endure. The last, Sharon, was the only child not endowed with a Chinese name which might outlast marriage.

My mother was once Italian. She met my father in a Chinese cafe called 'The Golden Star'. Under this sign of hope my parents consummated their love and loneliness. She learned to cook rice and stir-fry and put five spice powder in the spaghetti sauce. She understands Italian, but will not speak it except to correct my pronunciation in restaurants. Her maiden name was Marcon but she has been Mrs Woo Gong Lam for thirty six years.

The cultural and linguistic indeterminacy of my name suits me. In Europe, May means a time, the coming of spring. In China it is an adjective, a fine, utopian word like those lit up in neon outside Chinese restaurants: The Brilliant, The Excellent, The Lucky - or even The Golden Star. It is truly an auspicious name, a name to help number two daughter find her place in the world. Maybe.

still waters run deep

I WENT BACK TO THE CITY I grew up in. Bearing the imprint of all the other cities I have lived in and visited since. The street where our house used to be had disappeared. I spent a long, hot afternoon looking for it. When I finally found the place where it used to be, the houses had all gone and the street had been re-built in another image. But the shadows were still there; exactly as I remembered them.

A Woodcutter walked by a lake one night,
When the moon was full and beaming bright.
Smiling and singing, as he strolled along,
He glanced at the water; something was wrong.

There's been a lot of water under the bridge since then.

The photographer photographs only water. Nothing else. The gallery walls become huge walls of water. Falling down like rain.

I know this city. The pavements warped and split open by the hot, dry summers, the front yards full of cars washed and polished every weekend and the thwack of flyscreen doors as children run in and out.

The ancient Chinese saw cities as finite and built them in rectangles. Heaven they knew was unending, and therefore circular. In gardens they built arched bridges over ponds and streams, so that when the water level was just right, the bridge, together with its reflection, would appear to form a perfect circle.

The water bringing the sky to earth and the earth to the sky.

In Amsterdam The Photographer lived in an old warehouse above a canal. Every night before she went to sleep, she stood at the window and looked at the still, black water below. From Amsterdam she went to Venice. Water cities. Cities built on water. Who would dream a city built on water these days? The Photographer cries when she is far from water.

Floods of tears.

For deep in the lake, not up in the sky
Lay the pearly white moon from up on high.
'The moon's in the lake! I must get it out!'
The Woodcutter cried. And he started to shout.

In China the reflection of the moon in a lake is said to be the gateway to a mermaid's palace.

I know this city I grew up in, in pieces. All connected to particular events. To begin with I remember things, people and places: red plastic sandals, my best friend Joan, the beach. Then I add verbs to my list of nouns: to go, to go to the beach, to swim, to swim in the sea. But I didn't swim in the sea. I couldn't. I didn't know how. I didn't learn to swim until I was far away from that time.

Still waters, as they say, run deep.

In the south of Việt Nam the Mekong River ends its long journey from the mountains of Tibet; sliding into nine distributaries known as 'Dragon's Mouths' which, in turn, slide into the South China Sea. Places where fishing boats slip silently into the night to uncertain destinies on unknown shores.

By the banks of foreign rivers and along the shores of distant seas, The

Photographer takes notes, connects moments and images into a narrative that will never be completed.

'If we don't get it out the moon will drown!'
He cried, as he ran towards town.
'Come all you men, come you all and be brave
And save the poor moon from a watery grave!'

From Châu Đốc, The Photographer travels a narrow causeway to Tân Châu - the last town along the Mekong before Việt Nam becomes Cambodia. Houses balanced on spindly legs line the causeway, and a canal full of boats and floating homes runs along one side. On the other, the monsoon-swollen Mekong has burst out over a vast plain of rice fields. And the causeway seems to be leading out over an infinite sea - the only dry land for miles around. As far, as far as the eye can see.

I remember the back yard of our weather-board house. On hot, summer nights I'd lie in bed, the window open to the night. The moon lighting up the yard with an uncanny stillness.

All night they toiled to the Woodcutter's tune
And tried - in vain - to haul out the moon.
But the moon just lay there silvery-blue,
Sighing and shining; enjoying the view.

The chiaroscuro of water cities is like nothing else in the world. Opalescent buildings shimmering pink and gold above the water. Still waters moving in flickering reflections, in winding contours and concealed boundaries.

The ancient Chinese city of Suzhou was a walled rectangle surrounded by a wide canal, and symmetrically gridded with streets, alleys and smaller waterways. The old walls are mostly gone now, and the city has sprawled far beyond its original rectangle, but fragments of the ancient design remain. The white-washed walls of houses, outlined by brown wood doorways and balconies, present a continuous facade to the street. Sycamore trees arch over, casting dappled shadows onto the houses and the water below. Narrow alleys run between the streets and canals, and sometimes become footbridges over the water. And hidden behind the walls of Suzhou The Photographer discovers a world of zigzags and meanders, of shadows and reflections.

Still waters, still run deep.

When the sun came up at the break of day,
The moon breathed its last and slipped away.
For it wasn't the moon that fell in the lake,
But an image reflected. What a foolish mistake!

In an almost airless, dark brown shop I encounter - by chance - silent places I once knew. And silent people I have never known. In a shoe box of old photographs Tied up with string. People slipped in between the moment of action and the click of the camera.

And from the dark brown shop to a corner newsagent wedged in below a glass and concrete tower. Newspaper headlines scream in watery metaphors from behind rows of chocolate, raffle tickets and dusty magazines with curled corners. 'Flood of Boat People Feared.' 'New Wave of Refugees.' 'Rivers of Blood . . . '

On unfamiliar beaches, people are washed up in tides of hostile words.

When I was seven my days were filled with water. Running water. During the long summer holidays I'd run wet in my bathers from the backyard to the corner newsagent for an ice cream. Choc ices were my favourites. And then I'd run back to eat it under the sprinkler. The water and ice cream running down my face in sugary, white streams.

I dreamed whole worlds under the sprinkler that summer.

goin' 'ome

WE TRAVELLED ALONG MILES OF winding road. The hum of the car's motor lulled me off to sleep for a while. I saw visions of trees disappearing as the car seemed to eat up the roadway. I shut my eyes and dreamed I was a child again, listening to the raucous sound of those damn guinea fowls running around on the Mission at Box Ridge where I was born.

When I was only little I tried to learn how to ride a boy's bike. One day comin' down the hill full tilt, with my skinny legs tucked through the frame of the bike, I ended up crashin' into a lantana bush. When the grown-ups heard me cryin' they came and found me with my knees skint and a dirty face. Just then the car hit a rut in the road waking me from my slumber and dreams. 'Hooley dooley,' I yelled, sitting up straight. Pammy was chucklin'. 'That sure got ya going.' 'Yeah, I was in dreamland.'

Soon we were on the outskirts of Purfleet Mission at Taree. This was the place where my son-in-law came from. I remember we had visited his grandmother back in the seventies one Easter time. She was a dear old girl. She had chilli bushes growing around the side of her house and made deadly chutney and pickles. When we came into Taree the streets were busy with shoppers and there were lots of Kooris doing the rounds of the town. We called hello when they looked in our direction, wondering who we strangers were.

We travelled along steadily. The damn road was full of terrible potholes that looked only small but when you were close up they were real big and deep which caused the station wagon to bounce up as soon as we drove over them. 'Bloody road,' Pammy was cursing. 'Ya can't see the ruts until ya hit them, aye!' 'Yeah, they're terrible. No wonder there's a lot of accidents here.'

We were coming into a town called Maxville outside of Nambucca heads. 'I had a girlfriend when I first came down to Sydney in 1949. Her name was Evelyn Owens and she came from here, Pammy. Her granny lived in great Buckingham Street Redfern, that's how we met. Her father was a meat inspector. She was a gubba but a good friend. We used to go to the movie matinees on Saturdays. A whole lot of us kids used to sit on the steps of those flats and yarn each night after tea. There were Greeks, Kooris and Indians, as well as white kids, and we were all mates.' 'Yeah, some places were good,' Pammy said, 'though some weren't, aye?' 'No racism there then.'

The next place we were coming into was Coffs Harbour: banana country. 'Have you seen the big banana?' Pammy asked me. 'No, this is the first time I've ever been on this road in a car ever,' I told her. 'Wow, that's wonderful. So this is a grand tour for you, eh?' 'Sure is,' I answered.

We pulled into a garage and filled up with petrol and oil, then we drove on the outskirts of Nambucca. I spotted the big banana. 'We'll pull up and have a Devonshire tea, aye Ruby?' 'Yeah, that will be good.' But when we parked the car we found that the restaurant where you used to be able to get the teas had gone. 'Oh well, that's progress,' Pam said. 'Never mind, we'll find another one later on. You probably had to walk a long way to get to it.' I didn't feel like walking that much so we drove on and it wasn't long before we were on the outskirts of Grafton, still heading north towards McLean and Woodburn. It's a bloody long way to travel going home to my country. It was well worth it though, my childhood memories were not good ones but there were other memories that made all the difference to me.

Soon we were coming into Broadwater; from here we turned inland crossing the Richmond river over a big bridge. 'We're nearly home, not far to go now,' I called out, excitement showing in my voice. 'Yaroo! Yaroo!' Pam yelled. 'People will think I've got a mad woman in the car,' she said, laughing.

We came over a small hill, then I recognised some buildings: there was the church, then further on, the corner shop where we used to come from the Mission to buy things in those days long ago. We'd buy coconut ice-blocks, mild ones with flavourings in them, cool drinks, cherry cheer, when we had a few pennies to spend or were cashin' in cool drink bottles. We got tuppence each for draggin' them to the shop in a big chaff bag, even though it was a mile and a half to that damn shop! It was long way to struggle just for coconut ice-block! Memories – I was full of memories.

'This is the little corner shop we used to come to from the Mission, Pammy. There was a short-cut over the back through those houses,' I said, pointing. 'All those yards had loads of guava trees in them. We used to pinch them from the back lanes.' My stomach started to rumble, though it wasn't from hunger; it was excitement. I was goin' on worse than a little kid but the closer I came to this Mission I was born on, the more emotional I became. I could hardly contain my excitement and was fidgetin' around. 'Settle down, old girl,' Pammy told me. 'Settle down or you'll bust a gut!' 'Okay, okay. Take the next turn to the left at that road comin' up, it will take us to the hospital; then we go in round the back and we're nearly home to my real belongin' place, Pammy girl.'

On arriving at the front of the hospital I said: 'Pull up, Bub.' I just sat lost in my thoughts, gazing at the place for several minutes. Painful memories of a time when my people had one big room down the back with a sign on it which said 'Abos Only'. It was a segregated hospital then, I wonder if it still is. They were very racist here when I was a child.

'Come on, let's go, no good dwellin' on sorrow,' I said. We drove past the hospital and following the road, circled right round the back, past a very modern golf course. We didn't have far to go before the country became very familiar to me. We turned into a roadway right next to the cemetery and I knew we were nearly home to Box Ridge Mission.

The closer I came to it the stranger were the feelings I had. It was frightening at first but then I was eager to see this place 'cause the only memories I had of it were painful. Only this time I'd be seeing it through grown up eyes, not the eyes of a child. Before the gate was a big signpost which said 'Box Ridge Aboriginal Mission'. Pammy said she wanted to pull up and take photos of me in front of that deadly sign. 'Okay,' I said, gettin' out of the car.

Standing in front of the sign I had a good view of the Mission area; then it started to drizzle misty rain. I was standing with my feet placed firmly on the ground they hadn't touched for 48 years. My childhood visions remembered it as a big place. I was eight when I was here last, and looking at it now I realised it really wasn't that big. My eyes searched for the old school. Memories of sulpha and molasses poured down our throats every Monday morning . . . the long wooden tables and stools we sat on to eat meals . . . the old bell tower whose toll could be heard echoing across the common, summoning us to classes . . . the old vegie patch where we toiled growing things, pulling out weeds. The girls' garden was full of flowers: gerberas, zinnias, and roses, whose heady perfumes made us mission kids imagine we were in another world where all things are beautiful, where people laughed a lot, and didn't have a care in the world . . . . It wasn't like I'd imagined it. The big tennis court in the middle was gone. Anyway, after Pammy took the photos I told her I'd like to sit in the car for a while, my voice going quiet. 'I want to do some thinking, please.' 'Okay, I understand,' she said.

My eyes searched the paddocks where once tall millet grew, used for broom makin'. In the place where the old school house once stood, there was a modern brick home. I wondered what lucky Koori lived in that place! There was nothing so grand in my day. Then those places were old wooden houses, with wooden windows that were propped open with a stick! No running water, only tank water that was very precious and not to be wasted. Guinea fowl ran everywhere makin' a terrific racket with their loud calls. Kaa, Kaa, Kaa! And in winter the frost was white on the ground, like a white sheet covering all. It numbed our toes turning them pink when we crunched, crunched over it doing an errand. I remembered crossing a ploughed field when I was seven to buy some eggs at a farm house about three hundred yards over the back. I had a billy-can with a lid on it to carry them in. Crossing that field on the way back I nearly trod on a big black snake. When I ran to get away from it I fell, breaking all the eggs, for which I was belted and put to bed without any tea. They didn't suffer fools in those days. I looked towards the old common down the foot of the Mission which was on a small hill. In the old days when it rained we had to wade knee-deep in water into town each day to buy fresh bread. Us girls would tuck our dresses into our bloomers and wade all the way across - it was about five hundred yards over to the other side. When we got colds they'd dose us up with eucalyptus in a teaspoon of sugar and give us hot lemon drinks with aspros in them.

Us kids had no toys to play with. We were too poor, us old blackfellas, so we made our own games up. We had bike wheels without spokes. We'd run with a stick in the groove until it picked up speed, and boy could it go! For another game, we'd use sunshine milk tins filled with dirt. Poked a hole through it with a nail then threaded string or fine wire through it and clamp the lid on and wow, we had a steam roller!

I never did have the chance to come back until now. I'd had a family of my own to raise, mostly on my own, nine of them there were. They took some raisin' I can tell you! I did any kind of work I could get: fencin', burnin'-off, tree loppin', men's work, anything I could get to feed my hungry brood.

Although I was a trained clothing machinist, that was for city livin'; they don't got no rag trades in the country town, aye! It was with deep regret that I never had the chance to come home before now or to bring my kids and say 'Right here; I was born right here!' My mum had us all at home, no hospital deliveries for black women in those days.

'Come on, Ruby,' Pam said. 'Let's go, no good remembering all the hurts.' 'All right, Pammy, I'm sorry for takin' so long but I was lost in a world of my own, a long, long time ago.'

i look at a star

SUSAN LAURA SULLIVAN

i look at a star
things i couldn't draw in school
a 6 point star
one ▲ on another ▽
an 8
two circles on each other ⚬⚬ 8

NO NO NO
eight
8 is a line crossed over
curled up like coming down the
escalator on the wrong side of
the BIG store 8
NO NO NO
a star is
a star fish
5 points
crooked in water
gallop like horse

mrs Roki
teacher
she no like me
catholic
i see her in church
mrs Roki
i carry her books
mrs Roki
hello mrs Roki

i say when she takes communion
but she no like me
NO NO NO
she strikes the fear of God
into me

so
at home
i draw a triangle △ on a triangle ▽
a circle ◯ on a circle ◯
solid shapes
separate lines
and I see
I am
a star

swooping firebird

MONICA RASZEWSKI

A YEAR AFTER BARBARA'S DEATH, I dreamt that I was standing in Barbara's loungeroom. Barbara held a black and white photo which she wanted to show to me. I leaned forward and looked into the photo. A dark haired girl sitting under a pier on a beam of wood just above the water. The dark haired girl was Barbara at the age of ten. The girl sat side on, sulky, refusing to talk or to look at me. Finally the girl let herself fall headfirst into the water. The water was still. I lifted my head, stepped back and looked at the sixty year old Barbara standing next to me. Barbara pointed at the still water and said, 'I can always get her back.'

When I awoke after the dream I felt as if a letter I had been expecting had finally arrived.

On Friday morning, two days after the dream, I was alone in the office. I was separated from the public reading room by a heavy door, and I was separated from the senior Art Librarian by a wall of high bookshelves and filing cabinets.

The desk opposite mine was clear except for two stacks of neatly arranged files. I opened the top drawer of the neat desk and took out an opened packet of barley sugar. I pushed a lolly out of the paper packet without tearing it, put the lolly into my mouth and put the packet back.

I sat at my desk and opened my diary. There were clean spaces in between faint blue lines all the way from last Monday to the heavy blue line separating Friday from Saturday. I turned back to the beginning of the diary. The first two pages contained a map of the world. The planet Earth looked like a circle that had been squashed from above and below into an oval lying on its side. Most of Europe was coloured orange. I put my finger on Poland, the country my parents came from. I traced a journey with my finger that passed through Italy, over the Mediterranean Sea, through the tiny gap of the Suez Canal, across the Indian Ocean to where I guessed Fremantle was on the purple continent of Australia.

During my high school years I spent nearly every night of the school week in Barbara's spare room. I told my mother that Barbara's spare room was the best place for me to do my homework.
    The first time I went into the spare room I closed the door and sat at the desk without turning the lamp on. I put my books on the floor. A large globe of the world stood on the far corner of the desk. I pulled the globe towards me and slowly turned it around. I touched the raised surface of the mountain ranges of Asia. My finger made a track through the dust across the top part of Asia around to Europe and stopped at Poland.
    Poland was a deep pink. I wrote down the names of three cities: Warsaw, Lodz, and Krakow, on the inside of my exercise book. I wrote in the semi-darkness and I believed that while I sat in that room no one would ever disturb me, that even Barbara would forget I was in her house.

I turned over the pages of my diary and in the space for Friday wrote, 'Working on the Ashford collection.' I put on my grey dust coat and picked up my clipboard and notebook. I walked out of the office and down the stairs to the basement like an engineer about to make an inspection of an ocean liner's engine.
    Heather Ashford was a well known artist and collector of books who had left her book collection and papers to the library. When the library had received the donation the Art Librarian had walked into the office, pulled a chair up to my desk, sat on the edge of her seat and clasped her hands. Her eyes shone and her skin seemed smoother and younger as she told me about the donation. For a moment I had a picture of her as a seven year old girl about to receive a large Christmas present.

I rubbed my hands and put them on the desk. I imagined picking up a book with a scuffed leather binding, covered in dust. I turned the thick white pages. Each page had a hand coloured plate or steel etching of an ancient building, a temple, or statue that no longer existed because it had been ransacked or destroyed in war.

I was nine years old when I first visited Barbara. Barbara was a high school teacher and a painter who lived on her own. Her backyard joined my parents' backyard. The fence separating the two backyards had several gaps which my father was repairing during weekends. I used to squeeze through a gap in the fence after school and play at the end of Barbara's garden.

I had been squatting with my back to the house, digging a cave at the base of an old tree, when Barbara called out to me and asked me to come in. I followed Barbara through a dark corridor with low bookshelves into the loungeroom. The loungeroom walls were covered in pictures and an old crimson rug was spread on the floor. Books lined two sides of the room and almost touched the ceiling.

I wanted to read every book in the room.

The books from the Ashford donation had been placed on shelves in a corner of the basement. The exhibition catalogues and art magazines were kept in boxes nearby.

I stood on a low footstool in a corner of the basement and took down the books from the highest two shelves. I was working on a list of Heather Ashford's books and magazines. I wrote the title, author, edition, year and publisher of each book in a notebook, as well as any other information that future researchers and readers might find useful.

If an author or author's assistant came into the library and asked for any material related to Heather Ashford's life or work, I would be able to hand over my notebook together with the thick Heather Ashford file. Sometimes I imagined myself as the researcher sitting at the back of the reading room, drawing a map of the books listed in the notebook. The drawings would resemble old star maps with dotted lines linking the titles of books and authors and the paintings of Heather Ashford.

I got down from the stool and stacked old paperbacks on French art in even piles on the floor. I sat on the footstool and opened my notebook.

The year I turned fifteen, Barbara painted a bright red bird swooping into blue, yellow and green flames. She called the painting 'Swooping Firebird'. I walked backwards and forwards in front of the red bird. My sister, holding a half-filled glass of orange juice, followed me. The bird was about to crash into blue, yellow and green jungle. It reminded me of my sister's parrot. I hated my sister's parrot because it left its dung on the curtains and furniture. My mother did not mind the mess left by the parrot. She said that when she was a child she had always wanted a parrot but that it was too cold for parrots in Poland.

I bent forward to touch the thick paint on Barbara's painting. I felt a splash of liquid against my ankle. I jumped and pushed my sister back.

The first book in the pile on the basement floor was on Monet. It had been signed, dated, and annotated, 'Bought at the Exhibition of Modern Art. Town Hall. Melbourne, 1939.'

I wrote the title of the art exhibition next to the date 1939 and reread the entry. That was the year my mother was born and the year my mother's parents moved out of their house in Lodz and left for Warsaw, where they thought they would be safe from the war.

My grandmother, a young woman of twenty-two, carried a baby in a bundle of white bedding and my grandfather carried two suitcases. My grandmother wore a hat and a long coat buttoned up to her throat. She held the baby against her chest and followed her husband along a deserted street. They walked past factory chimney stacks and buildings which seemed hollow and threatened to collapse.

The woman holding the baby stopped for a moment. She looked ahead at her husband. He seemed to be struggling with the weight of the suitcases. His shoulders were hunched over and his grey coat looked too big for him. The woman was afraid that he would be stopped and questioned by soldiers. She waited for him to look back but he did not turn around.

I arranged the piles of books in lines around me. The lines of books looked like a model city of evenly spaced buildings. I sat in the central square and looked down on the city which spread across the concrete floor of the basement.

I saw the apartment building my mother had grown up in. The building had been built in 1910. My mother and her parents lived in an apartment on the third floor. Double doors from one room opened onto the next room and every window overlooked the courtyard. I walked through to the last room. A large double bed stood against the far wall. Large white feather pillows and a down quilt covered the bed like heaped-up snow. A metal crucifix hung over the bed. I stood at the window and looked down into the concrete courtyard. My mother was playing a ball game with a group of children. Her plaited hair swung behind her as she ran to catch the ball.

Barbara left Melbourne for London, the city she grew up in, six months before she died. In the last letter I received from her she wrote that she had finally found a place to stay while in England. She was moving into a flat on the fourth floor of an old building overlooking the sea on the Isle of Wight.
    I never saw the flat but I saw Barbara climbing up stone stairs carrying a crate of secondhand books, then stopping with one foot on the next step and taking a deep breath while balancing the box on her raised knee.
    Whenever I thought of Barbara dying I saw her carrying the crate of books and gasping for breath.

In the middle of the next pile of books I came across a novel called *The Visitors*. I opened the red marble paste-board cover. The novel had been written by Lucy Elliot and published by Chatto and Windus in London, in 1919. On the second page was a portrait of the author. The caption beneath the photo stated that the author was eleven years old when the photo was taken. I examined the self-satisfied smile, the neatly parted waves of hair, and the folded hands. On the blank page which faced the first page of text, was a small pencil illustration of a girl sitting under a table hemmed in by men's and women's legs. I examined the carefully drawn shoes and boots. I was certain that Heather Ashford had done the drawing as a child.
    The Visitors had no other illustrations. I got up and went back to the shelves. I took an armful of books and put them on the floor. I went backwards and forwards stripping the shelves, putting the books in stacks on the floor until the stacks of books formed a large semi-circle around my footstool. I sat in the middle of my nest of books.

Soon after Barbara's death I had received a letter which said that Barbara had left her books to me.

I carried eight empty cardboard boxes into Barbara's loungeroom. I took off my coat and marched up to the books as if I only had a few hours to spare. I skimmed the surface of spines with my finger, moving from left to right, lowering myself until I was on my hands and knees.

I knelt on the crimson rug and looked up.

From this kneeling position it seemed as if each book I looked at formed part of a circle. I wanted to dissect the bookcase section by section until each book's title, subject matter and the date when Barbara received or bought the book, were pinned down. I wanted to work out when Barbara read or studied or even flicked through the books on the shelves.

I packed Barbara's books into the cardboard boxes. When I arrived at my flat I pushed the boxes against my bedroom wall and covered them with a crimson cloth.

From time to time, while I was supposed to be doing my homework, I would creep out of Barbara's spare room into the corridor and crouch in front of the bookshelves. I would pick out books by Anaïs Nin or books about Minoa and ancient Greece and creep back into the spare room.

One night I pulled out a book on Polish painters and writers and took it into the spare room. Barbara had shown me the book several years ago and I had felt ashamed that I did not recognise any names or pictures. I had looked at the book in Barbara's hand but I did not touch it. In the spare room I carefully turned the pages of the book then read slowly, repeating the names of places and people out loud.

The evening before she left for England, Barbara showed me her latest paintings which were based on the patterns of the stars and planets. I walked around the loungeroom examining the intricate configurations of comets and stars and human figures. Barbara believed that the movements of the moon and planets affected facial contour and expression. She offered me a painting of a woman standing against an empty night sky. I asked Barbara if she would keep the painting for me until I found a place for it in my flat.

When Barbara left the room I went into the corridor and pulled out the book on Polish painters and writers. I put the book inside my coat, under my left arm, and pressed it into my side.

I picked up the next book in the Impressionist Series as if it were a building block. While I wrote down the title, date and author of the book I kept thinking about the crimson covered boxes lined up against my bedroom wall. I saw myself putting my hand into the first box and pulling out a book. I opened the front cover of the book. On the blank page facing the title page was a drawing of a young girl sitting on a pile of wooden crates.

in edith's case

PHILIPPA MOYLAN

EDITH SAT IN THE FRONT ROOM looking out of the window, seeing neither balcony nor passer-by. She saw instead the day that she and Arthur had found this place to live. Strange, the unfamiliar expression of interest that had passed across her son's face. Shall we take it, she had said, wanting to lure his interest even more by wrapping him up into the possibilities that danced around her question. And dizzy, elated, she had found herself rewarded by Arthur's quick, pleased glance.

Life in London revolved around this little house; not unlike a doll's house with its narrow hallway and high ceilings, miniature bedrooms and assorted spaces. Edith had decided that it was not its fairy story glamour that attracted Arthur here, for the chocolate-coloured roofs and icecream-frosted ceilings had lost their glazed finish, and the spirit of the lilies embossed on the fire place may have been preserved by their plaster casts but the detail evoked embalmment rather than first youth. Arthur's eyes, searching the hallways and rooms for something outside the centre of his self where every thought and action found its source and its return, appeared to be deciphering a code that was foreign to the familiar pattern from which he formulated his routines. If excited by his new surroundings he did not however step out of his enclosed world to meet them; instead he and the house were accomplices who, together, derived new patterns and rhythms which Edith was without the language to enter.

Performing the daily ritual of transforming dinner-table into work desk, furnishing it with her journalistic work, her diaries, dictionary and editorial notes, Edith experienced a gradual sense of relief. She began reverently, approaching the paid articles and book reviews, mentally subtracting her dependence on her husband's income. As she turned towards her own writing, the monotonous thud of Arthur's back knocking against the wall that separated mother from son stopped ringing in her ears and she entered the region of her tall story.

Not so tall that you could not find an intimate space on a window-seat in its tower, nor so narrow that you would be drowned out by those voices now barely audible from the sanctuary of the casements. In that tower Edith could analyse her observations made of that outer world, the distance a protection against the rising panic that had continually to be allayed. As always the figure of Hermione rose before her; Hermione, whose experience of a violent marriage, a child's death and the threat of incarceration still did not stamp out the clear glance that sought from every angle Edith's attention. A fragmentary sketch of Hermione's life covered her table, the loose style of her rounded letters belying Edith's need to bind her son into language. But the text of Hermione's Ernest could not be stitched so easily on to her son. The space between her tall story and the place where Arthur dwelt was divided by a channel that did not join son and mother, art and life, in blissful fusion, but instead marked out their separate positions. And increasingly Edith felt her position to be under siege, especially when the doctors turned away from Arthur and towards her, as if she was the object of their interrogation. To break down that mechanical clocklike rhythm of Arthur's life, in time with itself but at odds with virtually everything around it, would, Edith argued, be the moment of finding the source of and the cure for the boy's condition. But as the doctors were more concerned with picking away at the seams of Edith's carefully constructed sentences, her private fears grew larger, and soon there were only huge gaps in whose reflections she read the diagnosis before it was even decided: Arthur's condition was dysgenic; in some way she was responsible for his illness.

There is something safe about a completed piece of writing; I made myself a special pot of coffee and as I drank I gave way to the pleasure of the starched pages and their immaculate presentation. But safety is not a definitive force in times of doubt: the phantom ideas that had startled and then eluded me throughout my research were not substantiated by the grammatical assurance contained within these justified margins. Shrouded in the dead metaphors of my tribute to this nineteenth-century New Zealand writer lay the corpse of Edith.

So it was back to the computer screen. I read through every document that I had compiled about Edith Searle Grossmann and turned again to the finished article - this time on screen - and as time slipped and the words became less coherent I watched the shapes that once were letters. But out of those strange lines I sensed a figure jump from the page and now I could hear his footsteps outside the door as he roamed the corridor. It was safety I wanted now. I sought out the sentences and turns of phrase that were familiar to me but I had lost my way back in. My article had disappeared and the computer groaned with effort as if struggling to keep its memory intact. The figure outside pushed on the door and turned the handle against the lock's will. Help me Edith help me I repeated while the computer screen deployed its own invasion manoeuvres and alien configurations made their way into print. But as the letters took shape their form defied any font available. And so I followed the elaborate hand of Edith's writing and saw the figure of Hermione still wandering the sands long after the final pages of *In Revolt* had closed. The threat of incarceration dissipated and the law of the marriage-contract bent and collapsed in the furnace that bordered the plains where Hermione walked. But Hermione's freedom could not shield the heart whose desire to bleed life back into a dead child only gave intensity to the flames that ravaged law and love alike.

i

How we came to this no man's land, I wonder still. I sat in a narrow room, the five windows so small that the light shot through, pencil-thin and sharp. I colonized those five lines of light with the notes that sang in my head. The melody, aerobic, self-absorbed, flew between the bars of light. When it paused on a rest, it found itself surrounded, held in check by a myriad of voices. The invading notes fell like skittles, but regrouped as an army and took control of the stave. The sun moved across the building and the stave disappeared, but the invaders remained. Imprisoned within the range of a semitone, my theme came back to me through the drone of the intruders' voices, its melody thin and threadbare but persistent. I kept faith with it, invoking it, keeping it alive. But it is here that my story comes undone, for I cannot remember what happened to myself or the melody. Somewhere I lost days or weeks, and I remember waking here, the deafening drone of cicadas ringing in my ears.

ii
While we sit in silence, mute women, sharing a stick, one of us forms a word on sand, the other choosing a pivotal letter from where to launch the next word. The little stick-figure - vertical ABUSE - grows limbs; her right shoulder, formed from O[B]LIQUE, gives way to an arm: D[E]FAMED. A left leg runs away from the tip of ABUS[E] in an arabesque that reads INCARCERAT[E], spanning from the point of her toe, from I to the [E] of her cervix. Pulling hair gnashing teeth we make our terrible moves. One of our children is torn from limb to limb, FARN lodged inside the hip of the stick figure, NEST the hat on one of her two heads. We look at the words we have made and wonder why we have built the very prisons from which we have escaped.

iii
Pieces of sky, flies, parched twigs and leaves paraded before me. My bed was a woman's petticoat, its canopy a gum tree. Beside me knelt a woman, looking strangely out of place in this wild, hot space. She was not unfamiliar to me, yet I could not place her. I watched her face as she wiped mine with a damp cloth. Her tailored bodice clung to her chest in patches of sweat. 'You must be Miriam,' I said. 'No, I am Hermione,' she replied. But as the trees continued to fly before me, the ground losing its hold and breaking away from under us, dry clay now treacherous mud, it was Miriam I called to: 'I see you have been cast away from your community and forced to roam the wilderness these seven days. I am sorry.' But Hermione, not Miriam, returned my gaze and I knew my fever was gone. I had difficulty looking at her directly, she whom I had made a living sacrifice. I brought you into being, but your story was always already there. 'We are the aberrant women,' said Hermione quickly, defiantly.

iv
When we return across the border, we may fade, our selves assimilating themselves to our husbands, for legally, marriage has made us one with them, and they are that one. My husband's body still hangs around

me like a shroud, the hot wind assailing my senses as his breath brushes against my mouth. I bury my head in my armpit, inhale, but he holds fast to me, a corset. I scrub the dress in the river, but still a terrain can be mapped where his body has been. Unlathered, without the mild, pure properties of soap, the garment is immersed in water again and again; I work it between my fingers, but it only wears away the skin on my knuckles. I am riddled with him. Edith approaches and leads me away from the river. We lay the dress out to dry across the rocks. Avoid drying in direct sunlight, warm iron; I almost laugh.

v
I dreamed that you and I were being followed, even in this desolate place. The intruder was close by; I heard his approach. I woke you and we ran, and soon I realised that neither rock nor scrub obstructed our way. Beneath our feet was an infinite book which spread out before us. Your feet travelled over its margin and mine the lines of text. My eyes followed the figurations on the page until I felt sand between my toes and saw how it obscured the letters of each word until the words were gone, and then the page as well. Ankle-deep in water, we stood, looking out towards a proliferation of paths furrowed out in the sand ahead; we had only to choose which one/s to take.

vi
When we return across the border, we must carry before us that image of dancing flame that laces the horizon. Let us leave behind these impassive rocks, chiselled away by sea, bled dry by wind. Look instead towards those distant boughs, once dry and phthesic, now incandescent in that yellow crimson flame. It is from this moment that we must draw our strength, keeping alive that ancient bush, aglow but unconsumed by fire, its incense our benediction, its ardour our call to battle.

vii
I looked back across the white expanse and could see our intruder in the distance. His body, small and agitated, struggled to mount the tip of the book's spine, but the pages that had spread out before us like a plain, now rose and swelled, and the intruder was lost from view. Silently the pages heaved towards each other, filaments coming together, ending in a final embrace: a marble column. As if suspended

there also, we waited, but no recalcitrant figure emerged from the peripheries of the imposing monument. We moved onwards, and as we walked I saw again the writing on those pages, and it was familiar to me. I relayed to you my thoughts and we conceived of that looming figure, forced to roam the papyrus leaves of this expansive tome. We who were once the objects of his pursuit, and who were now the unwitting architects of his demise, felt our pleasure paralyzed only in the margin of fear that he might decipher our hieratic text and reinscribe his own meanings. So it was between these poles of èlan and dread, and through the labyrinth of paths before us, that we charted our journey from the bowels of the wilderness.

Edith Searle Grossmann (1863-1931) grew up in Beechworth, Victoria. In 1878 she moved with her family to New Zealand. After completing her MA, Edith worked as teacher, journalist and novelist; her various writings address feminist, social and environmental issues.

once i was fou roux's lover

OR RATHER I LOVED LOOPY RED as I liked to call Vincent Van Gogh. Not Fou Roux as the Arlesian children chanted after the ear episode. Not mad. But not straight either. Loopy.

From my first meeting with Vincent it was irreversible. I was gone, stretched, dispersed, concentrated into pockets of intensity, re-dispersed. I laughed with the boom in my blood, the ricochet of troubled structure through my world. Nothing would stay put any more. My vision was jolted into supreme, slow sight. Immobile, I was also capable of great acceleration. My eyes grew fingers again. I saw shadow as becoming-light. Things processed me in their growth. I was seeing though a new kind of blindness. Perhaps the violence of illumination had detached my retinas. I was seeing multiply, loopily; I was surely cross-eyed.

After this I could never be straight, see straight.

I was Loopy Red's lover.

He was dead but I nursed him. I rocked for his passion. It could have been a sick cat, a dead flower, but it wasn't. It was Loopy Red. I didn't know or care whether he'd been a premature ejaculator or had too much of an arctic sear in those green eyes. It was never too much. He was a touching painter, literally, and I was in love with him. I was going to be a loopy red painter.

I was nine when I first found him in my aunt's loungeroom, on the rack of the blond wood table, under the glass. He was sleeping there with the calmer, more sumptuous Gauguin. I knew then why Gauguin hadn't stayed on at Arles in the Yellow House. Gauguin was a good housekeeper, kept his palette in order. Loopy Red had always been too much. As he looked at a plane tree he could feel the sap moving subcortically through him. As he looked at a lopped plane tree, he haemorrhaged, and re-sprouted. The sky was a whorled jubilation in his head.

I never forgot the gardenia in the shallow bowl my grandmother had placed on the glass. Inside this becalmed circle, limpidity made a scandal of his clamorous heart. But looking into the gardenia's perfumed flesh I found the white sky with the sense of gold beating behind it. I was sunstruck in my straw hat. I walked straight out of my picture window, along convulsive walls, through the flamboyant grass. Flowers flickered their little tongues at the palm of my hand, I felt the weight and the acid dampness of a clod of clay. I let my fingers bog and glue with it. I was Loopy Red's lover. I could have stayed in the ploughed field, between the almond trees for ever. I rolled and opened, greedy for every kind of contact. I was all finger, footsole, palm and tongue. My skin developed and multiplied its demon surfaces. I felt each petal-fall acutely, as a discrete event. I was kissed and kissing; I was inside-out.

For years I tracked him back from Arles to the taciturn town in Belgium. I came to the little miner's hut where the young pastor had practised his martyrdom. Already I could hear the Arlesian children chanting Fou Roux Fou Roux, which meant Loopy Red. I put my cheek to the stone, feeling in each pore the puncture of the wind's syringe, and on my tongue the sour taste of coal dust. There, with his face to the wall, I saw my Red, his body blue with the cold. I saw how gaunt his buttocks were and then wondered if *gaunt* were only for faces. He'd given up his clothes of course, having flung them to the miners. The oil lamp flickered a blue reply to his skin, a rehearsal for the Potato Eaters. The peasants with their sunken cheekbones didn't waste words. For the moment I saw them glancing from behind his eyelids. He carried the potato eaters protectively although they didn't want his charity either. He was shivering in his litter bed. I took some lumps of coal from my apron pocket, stoked the fire. We didn't need to speak. I lay down next to him, fingered his rib-cage as I might the strings of a guitar, wishing I could play the instrument. He accepted me, under-age though I was. A century too late. Loopy Red and I cradled one another. We warmed the black room with our unevenly shared breath. We found the spectrum of colours in the darkness. I felt the delicacy of his God as my fingers explored his shoulder, and his ignited my hair.

stationmaster

LINDA MARIE WALKER

The stationmaster's lamp grated on the morning.
(Patrick White, *The Solid Mandala*)[1]

1. ROMANCE

Oh . . . we passed the maroon walls unswayed by the ancient crockery in the pale light of the glass cases, and you whose name is unspeakable stayed close. A part of me was falling into a part of you, and you were delicate, fine finc lines of speech, low and melting and I could not then nor can I now faithfully remember . . . . On and on I talked while wishing to speak in waltz-time like the dark sky above the pine tree which was the bottom of a stormy sea when we stared at the cones poised to drop and the wind came in great waves still warm and we expected rain and sought shelter but the sun came out. I was not subtle like you, your words are subtle; your smile bare. I walked faster, you fell behind and made me speak and that part of me that was falling into that part of you turned, and I was touched enough to name it home, call my body home, and I said it's a cradle, I am held and safe from the outside, but you did not caress me, except perhaps by offering that drink. You said you saw me only when I spoke, and I became sound. Sharp as glass you entered, just as the man with the book said: the monument is dead! Next, from across the room you poured inside to a lake, clear familiar water, and I heard the morning bells, a holy hollow, if I could join you I'd . . . well . . . . And that's that, history turned in a second, history in my reflection. You seemed thin and weary. I couldn't fix your face even when you said, there is much to do, and I said, does that worry you, and you said no, and I said (because I was lost in your wrong answer), then can you see?

There is fear/are warm shivers in my body like a trapped bird/wary birds, I must walk far before it dies/they die. I am usually more vigilant.

I was on a train to somewhere days away, to a calm autumn, when I first saw the stationmaster. Slowly passing a platform a man, twice my age, say, stood under lamplight and watched as I watched him until I was again by a window in moving night country. He was more than his sign: The Stationmaster. A tracing on my skin, absolute as rain (as it was raining). Oh . . . and you were willing for me to drink, while others ate. I turned, threads, each word bound by skin, guarding me in your sight. My moth body coloured purple instead of pale pale blue, bending this way and that, bone. Once, waiting in the traffic, a man waved from a balcony, and the day opened, glistening, and I was struck. Another time, trapped in a car, a man freed me, and made me stand. And then into the room of long covered windows came all the stationmasters, together, and at that moment I needed hushed air, but instead you handed me a drink and told me of a woman who built museums of glass walls. Extraordinary how your shoulders sloped (like mine), your hands curled (like mine). I keep you alive, despite my cautious nature.

The day of meeting is distant. I overlooked your leaving; I believed it a beginning; as if I'd gain your name. A red coat hangs on the door, feathers escape from a cushion, the window reminds me of an old bridge. Its curved approach deserving wide steps, as if leading from a vault or a tomb, thirty splendoured steps each with balustrades and spheres balancing on pedestals. Anticipatory steps, giant stairs. And behind: stars, and a clear cold sky. Softly lit stairs. The stationmaster is by the lake, its shallow edges murmur. I own a perfect cup, exact against my lips, white, and that is that. The stationmaster is that cup, a shape. I hear you speak, I concentrate, but I can't reach your flesh.

We went to a room with dark wood, and your fingers that were mine were still yours, I stood in the doorway. You beside me, in front, behind, embraced by this surveillance, saturated. This warrants a lengthy report, twenty pages say, as each slight movement of mine (and yours) is (I am sure) a sort of justice, disrupted/disputed vision. Am I ill, for instance, can I manoeuvre against my will, against every single chore I do, like wake, wash and weed? The stationmaster says, smoothly: I wonder if a train trip would help. Of course, I say. This is nature, a plain, land in all directions green, brown, and gold, a thin black horizon. I am looking at the bridge, secretly, with my hands and feet, and by my bare neck. It is a pavilion for footsteps. It is a passage, a memorial, and my function, as a speaker, is to be attentive, as if I am one not two spaces. Well, well, well what tendencies . . . .

I want a room where I can stare at you all over my skin. This room must be the quality of sand, the warm liquid of harmony, an enunciation, a stain. And I am worried; my garden is wilting, tiny seedlings are yellowing under geraniums and nasturtiums. I care now and then, early morning perhaps, or as I undress. I say to you (the stationmaster) use your tongue like fingers. And you look down, I see you look down, then up, should I signal to you across the table, would you signal back? You stay behind me, gazing, while I guide us along a wharf in cool air. I wish my face was veiled, in mourning, with an inner chamber, chilled, late, listening to bells on a Sunday morning (I watch every balcony, I long for an accident).

Your appearances have followed bells, my romance: walking, the streets his corridors; this means a dark tradition: a tangible consistency, bread. Mouth to mouth, you've (I've) only your words, all that's left; all that ever was, you say.

The city is old, the mauve night creeps below the tall glass buildings showering the evenings with quiet. The city gathers in his hallway, he is shadow, shuffling, often breathless. This is too too much; yet I plot to map a site of crime, of sin. I am not anxious to leave well enough alone, to forfeit the carnal tense. That is, I am purple and not blue, wilful and not just amorous. And so I scheme to meet by the sea, to write across a table, to read aloud, as it is speech which stretches over sodden ground.

2. BURNING

Memory: I am in a red coat, someone is watching. I am burning. My arms and legs and back are melting, sweat forms on my eyelids and above my mouth. My nose runs, my ears ring, my heart skips, hollow as a cave. I listen to the night birds call in the cool early air, a single repeated note, and I recollect the smoke and dark of a different city foreign to the stationmaster, where I almost stayed, half lost in its wet light. I thought the stationmaster might visit that city, there were hundreds of trains. I expected him, or someone like him, and he came. This time in a book with a name I could have easily mistaken for a cry, or the colour of a sea, even a rare animal, perhaps the architecture of a lost culture. The dawn has arrived, I've tied back the curtains, I'd be sleeping except for the heat under my skin and the sly lingering ripples pinning my eyes open. I don't know what my body is becoming, but it's something I've never been. Up until he was introduced I could feel his breath. 'Unni,' said the General, and the man turned and she thought: how tall he is, and then: how dark he is. She shook hands, her hand disappeared into his.' [2] I was her, or she was me. Finally, as it was necessary, I travelled to that city, not to search for him, but to see what he had seen, stand on the same verandah. This body was, then, cooler, more cheerful, painless, it could sleep, it was more tacit. I knew Unni would not recognise me. I would never hear his voice or feel his hand on my shoulder, he would never pull me to my feet.

I leave you at the bottom of the steps; we had walked through a famous plaza, watched the circling water beneath the silver statue. We'd sat in a cafe and you'd said, I am disappointed, and the words came ghostly, from your lungs, slow and thick. You could have been saying something completely different, still, I want to scream, and this heat under my skin moves as a million worms from my feet to my eyes. And whereas I was cool in a shirt suddenly I am pulling my arms free from these rhythmic beatings: the body is strict. And then, instantly, cold as ice. I could (soon) burst into flame, a matter of ashes. I don't want sound, I am passing on, a not so slow passage. Unni is tall and brown, a fleeting lover, sort of ethical (heavens). Just after he is introduced by the General there's a light shower of rain, the dust settles, a good omen, a wedding begins; like moths around a lovely flame someone murmurs, later he, as a hero would, tosses a coin (soundlessly) up and down: 'His voice was very deep, low pitched like the lowest tone of a bell, it's very dark honey, it's like being under the shade of an enormous tree in a hot noon, a dark voice, this voice can never shout, she looked down at her arm on the piano lid and wondered, there was fine gooseflesh upon it.'[3]

I sweep up my peeled skin from beneath the chair. It is a very white day. There are no flowers in my garden now. The air is too dry to breathe. The white day goes on and on, a tiny breeze moves the vine. I followed you, pointing to the small square windows. My neck ached from nodding. And the heat came.

I woke one morning without the colour of your hair. But I looked the same, my hands, breasts, thighs, legs, feet. I was calmer. My skin crackled. I walked up and down, looking at the pavement, and the soft grass. By evening I could feel each heart beat, could watch my hands throb, and then I slept.

Morning (again and again), and grateful I see my red coat behind the door, all that remains of the stationmaster, the pleasure of his company. The sea will take him, crash his body on the reef. I may never cross his streets again. The day is cooler, yellow rather than white, and I can barely raise my head to sip the water on the table by the bed. I don't want to read to the stationmaster anymore, nor hear him read to me. Unni would not care for his city; his delight in facades would make him think your speech earnest, and he'd stand still, amazed at your belief, his eyes glazed, and toss his coin (soundlessly). His old and mouldy city crumbles, the smell of rot tangible. The stone gutters green with moss.

And then I remember us furtively sitting in a cafe. The day was wet and we watched the roads flood. Planes flew low, people marched, horses paraded. You never asked me questions, not even about my house. Unni lives in the mountains. You are not a mountain man. I told you about Unni, a long story for me; you laid your head on the table beside the white cup. It was the only time I persisted. I said (and at this point it had not struck me that I had already left you for him, I meant you to hear me, endorse the effort it would take (in this heat) to put him into words, as I was often breathless; you never saw my red skin, my damp hair, the brown creases on my hands, the softness of my fingernails, my wounded ankles, my black toes; at the time I was conveying an incident, like something I'd seen or heard, a fragment that could alert you to me, outline my character; all of these wishes much too fantastic for you, instead of revelation, you heard sound which served as caption, indecent words) . . . . I said: Unni was waiting for her, for me, in the dark on the steps of the bungalow she was about to move into, it belonged to him, she called his name and he said yes; she said, how did you know I would come here; and he said, one guesses; he had brought two of the General's trusted servants for her; they will look after you and this place, bring you hot water, prepare lunch under the walnut tree where you can look at the mountains, he said, one day you will ask me to have tea here with you; she sat on the step, he leaned against the door and began to toss something up and down (soundlessly); is that a coin, she said; an old coin, a charm, I use it when I am thinking, he said; I left the keys to the bungalow in the hotel, she said; I have a duplicate set, he said, I will let the servants in, as they will live here too, now shall we go to the temple; he took off his leather jacket and put it around her shoulders, he wore a soft woollen jumper; you think of everything, she said; almost, he said; then he took her hand and said, come, let me guide you. [4]

As I finished the heat pierced my head and I sat there, waiting, and saw myself pick up a sword and sever my feet.

3. WAITING

I stayed in that other city a year, in a large room with painted parrots on the walls, and sat beneath an old walnut tree in the grounds outside. I did not see Unni, or hear his voice, and now there is a new character. I thought I was sleeping. He said, we are in a cafe, there is coffee on the table, the air coming through the doorway is cold. He laughs (unpleasantly, I note). I don't want to struggle out, I say. The second body comes and goes, it's light as air, untouched, nervous and nauseous. He is not a stationmaster, he is not a hero either, I didn't read him, nor did he hand me water.

This time the man is (truly) out of reach, yet so near that he has disappeared from the roads and staircases. In this city there is no point or pleasure in descriptions or comparisons, this is the other's revenge, as it can not be other than itself, one street with the next, one building with its neighbour, a road with its footpath, a garden with its clocktower. A joke against the symmetry of the stationmaster's quest. And against the bits of writing he sought (and I loved), so lovely in their sense, and warming. And I am charmed. But the other city was more tangible than this one that I move in daily, its soft trees without perfume. My body is pressed flat, storing words, ones of little interest, but that are rare, and essential somewhere else. In that other city. It's a risky business. I sit in my big lounge chair and you come out of the shadows and sit in a wide soft brown chair opposite, you wear a white hat, you look writerly (feigning dignity). You are silent for several minutes We meet again, you say. I don't know if this is satisfactory, I reply. You cross your legs. The room is dim. Some light is coming from a window behind me. Behind you the wall is black. Your clothes are thin and loose around your body. You say, pull your chair closer. But this is futile, what possible honour will I know. He can't console me. There is a tiny moon tonight. It has rained again, every day it rains, then the sun shines, and it rains again. The stationmaster is probably huddled in a doorway thinking of the flat roofs across from him, planning a speech. I have no will to rise from the chair and walk to the bed. Every movement in this city is iron, yet I am polite. I wash my towels. And the rain begins. From my kitchen window I watch, and wonder if the red coat would drip like blood. And remember the heat that could come any moment, as if already here. Can you see me yet, you say. I say, you could be anyone. And you lean forward into the light. Your eyes are not as old as I'd expected. I'll tell you what it's like in the other city, I say; he seems pleased, surprised even. Over there the air is cold in December and all around the mountains faintly rise and rise through mist, sparkle between swift cloud breaks, often at dawn, and are red or yellow, even purple. It's a steamy musty place, even in the dark nights, even when the heavy sky drops to the chimney-tops. Out under the walnut tree the city sounds were muffled by the high stone wall. Sometimes I walked to the gateway to watch the white traffic and the white dust. I walked to see the fabrics, and the books. I walked back to sleep in the parrot room. There is nowhere to walk here, the paths are straight and hard, and when I go to my gate there are no animals, no wild flowers, no burning piles of leaves, no clothes drying on fences, no fountains, shrines, strong sweet tea. The high blue sky hasn't a single cloud. The rain falls from a summer sky. I can't understand your patience, it seems you will sit there a long time, forever even. Can I get you anything, I say. Then you start speaking like the rain. I'm amused at first, think of other things. Pretend I'm brave. Keep my back straight, my head up, when I sense the heat's return. It passes. When will the wind stop, you say. I hear tapping on my window, but it's rain again. The sun is out too, the towels would have been dry. There, I say, you can't help me there. Rain's rain, he says. I stood up, walked out, and slammed the door. There was no one anywhere. I gathered dry branches from the bushes and built a fire, and sat for an hour in the flickering light. No one came. When I closed my eyes he was still there, waiting but not troubling me. From my gate a few lights glowed in windows. In that other city I could lean on the wall as if to meet a friend, a woman who I'd perhaps known all my life who had also come to live leisurely near the mountains. I felt the heat again, or its phantom, and wondered if I had changed shape.

The fire is a night sail, the wind comes up and ash floats about. I could be facing the sea for all that is visible beyond the warmth. The flames are out, the street-light flashes on and off. I turn to my rooms, each of them empty, no music playing. This admission, that someone sits in a chair leaves me no option. He puts his hat back on. I am listening to footsteps somewhere out in the street.

I pray the heat will stay away, as he stands to rearrange his clothes, takes off his shining black shoes, and says: you'll be dead in bed one summer morning. He seems upset so I say: beyond the lakes there were fields of flowers, thousands of yellow *Nomocharis oxypetala* and some blue *Nomocharis nana*, and two kinds of geraniums, and a blue delphinium, and the wide flat amethyst blue *Polemonium caeruleum*, and a stream with cynoglossum in drifts beside it, and under an overhanging rock a single blue poppy, a pink rose and a bush rhododendron; and on the breeze was thyme-like scent, and I collected blooms and pressed them between the pages of heavy books, and hundreds of seeds which I sorted into small coloured glass jars which lined the mantlepiece.

The woman who'd once owned the parrot room said the bottles belonged to a man who'd lived in the room before me, who'd come to the city to gather a specimen of every flower in the field, he'd stayed ten years, and they were his parrots, she showed me his book and he had written: 'So for the next sunny hour or two we rested there or filled envelopes with seeds, and what better way is there of spending an autumn afternoon on a hillside? Which would you prefer: a flower in your garden or a mouldering head on your wall?' [5]

4. METHOD

I am building a stone wall around my rooms. I have built walls before, so far so good. The sky lately has deepened; promising a storm, snow and wind. I am learning method, focus, barrenness, a vista of yellow deserts, of blue treeless hills, a picturesque void; countryside. I go out to tell my wall that patience is a virtue. My breath hisses. I stop and add another layer of stone, it is well above my head. I stand for an hour or two, without a single thought (heaven(s)); the sun shone hard today and with a sea breeze. I swear my innocence. The vines cover this ordinary city, bare by winter; I deny everything. I rush into routine, to be hemmed in, no voice, no master. The rooms are often friendly: to write of one of them I'd begin: it is orderly, things are in their rightful place. I look at the wall outside, to placate the heat, save my skin. The days when masses of inky clouds hurtle across are best for the wall, then I see the other city, but only by degree, I am practising living where I am. I sweep, I sweep well, thoroughly, thoughtfully, sweeping halves my time. Sometimes I hear a child call, a bird rustle the leaves, a truck pass, a siren wail, and then quiet again, until the roof creaks or a grape drops. I come in from the wall and take the jars from a cabinet and with hot soapy water scrub the oily layer off the white boards. When the rain clears I leave the yard to gather more stones. I weed the garden and decide that a slow journey is a safe bet. The train weaving through the mountains with the rhododendron forests in bloom takes up a morning, I wake near the blue wheelbarrow. I build the whole afternoon. I am succumbing, slipping into the stones, I am becoming stone, indeed wall. I persist though, drop by drop, and stand inside my front door, my hand on the silver handle, and admire the tops of the wattle trees above the wall, their yellow flowers breaking open. The walnut tree I sat beneath was more than a century old, and the dish Martha served for supper (as she called it) was made with pickled green vegetables - and crushed walnut shells. Perhaps I don't need the wall ... but it is evidence, and peace. There is also another prospect: heat. I find myself lying on the bed: I'd been at the residency opposite the parrot room where the General spoke one morning to Martha (who'd once owned the room); she wore a red flannel dressing gown and he a lounge suit with a pink flannel band; he said, according to my best information Vassili will soon be out of jail; how splendid, said Martha; happiness filled the large room, and the dark marble floor shone as if wet, and the charm of the moment in the early light was frozen and profound for no discernible reason. [6] I imagine a landscape of grey-silver silk, a long way from my rooms. There is no white curtain billowing in the breeze. I've begun to hang pictures in my rooms. I smell smoke, and am lulled into long rests beside the back door beneath the wet towels, and hear a padding sound, someone walking, sounds about right. I've noticed a white lampshade, and turned it on.

1. Penguin 1977, p 41.
2. Han Suyin, *The Mountain Is Young* (The Book Club, London, 1958), p 87.
3. *Ibid*.
4. *Ibid*, p 155-157.
5. F S Smythe, *The Valley of Flowers* (Hodder And Stoughton, London, 1947), p. 285.
6. H Suyin, *ibid*, p 138.

in a shoebox packed with cotton wool

WHEN I WAS BORN I WAS CARRIED around in a shoebox packed with cotton wool. I faced death then. I am ready now.

My body shudders, then sinks into the mattress. Bloodless lips, wrinkle curled, droop to my chin. A ceaseless veil of energy spews from my head, slapping the casement of the bed, oozing into metal. If my hands could only farewell this ebbing lifeforce. But drug bloated fingers are inactive, unresponsive.

A figure is beckoning from the end of the bed.
I'm coming mother. Where's Charlie, is he there?
The shape withers, vibrating through my consciousness.

Yes, I know about him. All my childhood I've known about Charlie. Did you think it was a secret. You with your despair and disappointment. You with your fragmented melancholy. You who made me an immutable presence in shadow.

    I found out from others. Tales, you know. Outback gossip. Thought I couldn't hear their croaking tongues. Thought I couldn't see their pointed pious pity. Well it's my secret now. Charlie is my movie star. My soap opera.

I   Horse hoofs scurry dust in a frenzied willy willy and Charlie silhouettes the skyline. Brown swirls map his face. Charlie the Dogger, passing through with his net of dingo scalps.

II Beth and Charlie make love, devouring each other like quicksand.

III Jim returns. Accepts his wife's loneliness with noble Christian fervour.

IV Edie arrives, prematurely, so small she is carried around in a shoebox packed with cotton wool.

A fine man Jim, they say, accepting Edie as one of his own, not treating her differently. In hushed tones they whisper, she's special, you know.

What's special? I ask my mother.
   Beth's fingertips move from tearstained cheeks to calm the nest of my curls, leaving sticky watery marks across my forehead. Darling, it's when a person is so dear to you, you want them close by you all the time.
   Beth draws me close and I am satisfied.

Scene One through Four
Rerun

I sometimes think that I'm to blame for it all, says Beth.
   Gwen is seated across from Beth, soft faced, folds of flesh propping up her frame. Warm, comforting, lumpy Aunt Gwen.
   Oh, Gwennie, if I hadn't tried to lose her . . . that's what brought her on early, I'm sure of it. I just can't shake off the feeling of horror. That knife edge flaying flesh and somewhere in the depths my little Edie's face.
   Beth catches her face in her hands. Aunt Gwen's fingers reach out and stroke Beth's hair, lingering, replacing each strand as it rhythmically tumbles onto the table.
   Beth, you must stop torturing yourself. That's all in the past now. Edie dotes on you, she doesn't blame you. God, Edie doesn't even

know. So give it away love. Stop letting it cloud your life. You don't have to spend each waking moment blaming yourself for something that can't be changed. Besides, everyone should have at least three torrid affairs in their life. It's part of life, Beth. Edie's part of life.

Five-year-old Edie overhears, watches, works out The Plan. It's simple really. Her eyes will tell her mother. She stares at Beth every opportunity, blanking out expression, so only her gaze remains, searing into her mother's being, willing her mother to read the love burning in her eyes. Edie forbids her eyelids to droop. Soon her mother will have to believe that Edie loves her.

Beth was always obsessive about feather pillows. When I was three, my eardrum was pierced by a feather that worked its way from the cover. Feather pillow. Mismatched beads. Whistles. Voices. Fading in and out of dimness.

I dream. I am a perenti, a large lizard, lying dead beneath a log. They find me and break my legs. Each one snapped. Hurriedly. Efficiently. Fearful of the claws still able to embed themselves into arms or legs.

This is what death is like.

Here in this hospital.
This hostile hospital bed with this horrible pillow.
Reassuring voices fading into dimness.
Moving from first to third person.
From present to past.

I've faced death before.

It was me who walked the five miles to Aunt Gwen's house, hysterical, tears scalding barefooted blisters. Aunt Gwen stroked my cheek. We went together to lay Beth out, but I ran off. I remember the feel of dank soil in the irrigation ditch. Aunt Gwen sat next to me, hands locked around knees, rocking through my grief. I feel those paroxysms of anguish ripping through my stomach, gushing from my throat, chilling air.

I saw mother eventually. Gnarled fingers uncurled. Languid mouth a thin slit. Slate grey strands of hair wisped around the mass of bones, no longer resembling the curly softness that was mother. But the eyes held me. Their haunted, darting look replaced by the transfixed look I'd willed on her for all my years. In death mother had understood, had returned my gaze of love. The Plan worked, finally.

But there is still Jim.
Fine man Jim.
Jim, who calls me his special little Edie.
Jim, who never needs proof.
Jim, who remains while Charlie hustles off into the Depression sunset.
While Beth dies.
While Gwen dies.

Now there is only Jim and me. Jim who remains in despair, becoming more difficult to decipher. Jim who can't manage without Beth. Grieving for Beth, absorbing, consuming my mind with his grief. Like Uluru absorbs bushmen's memories.

I am only a memory now.

You're weak, I accuse Jim, almost making him go away. Him and his brain raping grief.
    I cut up tomatoes, slicing easily through the skin and watch Jim clutching Beth's scarf to his face, breathing in her lavender smell.
    I don't want to smell your sadness, Jim. I don't want to hear you cry into the depths of the night.
    The knife goes into Jim easily too. Like garlic lightly rubbed along the base of a salad bowl, seeping only the slightest blood juice.
    I look at Jim, bloodied Jim.
    And try to remember why I want him to go away.

But blackness is blighting thought.

You're Doggers like Charlie, scalping me with your electrodes and wires.

A fine man Jim, they whisper. She's special though, you know. And their tone is hushed and repulsed.

There's no one left to call me special now.
Mother's dead. Gwen's dead. Is Jim dead too?

I am three
I am five
I am
Only a memory now
Only me
Only Edie

And somewhere in the depths is my face.

eight-eighty-89

1

A shrinking of asphalt
a slight tremor in blood and sap
before the fall;
in Sydney and San Francisco
seabirds accommodating traffic
in a fog of fumes and seaspray
along crowded wharves,
Chinatown's familiar foreign smells
and clash of utensils
hang in the air
like the saxophones of soloists
practising in empty bars.

2

Cameramen in helicopters
watch from the sky
as the top deck of freeway eight eighty
buckles and breaks
leaving one woman stranded
on the wrong side of her destination.

For her everything has stopped,
the noise, the movement,
the moment
fast frozen.

She's alone with a single thought.
Ramming the little Corvette into reverse
she revs the engine so hard
you imagine you can hear it
over the noise of the helicopter
that's hovering there,
twelve and a half hours away.

She closes her eyes
puts her foot down all the way
and surges forward;
she flies over the wreckage-filled abyss,
and falls short.

She wasn't an actress
who could do her own stunts,
but she knew where she was going.
After the looting and the heroism
the bars fill up
and everyone else
takes the long way home.

what a waste

When I hear the trains go by, it sounds like work. They pay you to die, slowly, in a swamp of inertia. They're so nice you're bored. their second-rate marriages. Yeah sure you're *going* to. Their hopes muggy like the air-conditioning. And yet they're human. Love swells at half past three before you go home and you're contented. Contentment presses up its grey shield. You look out grey windows at a blue sky. The trains crash down each layer of the station. Feet jamming the escalator's steel comb. The smell of dissipated energy, of despair, smothering its giftshop hand over you. Noise swills inside the head. Faces smile over their grey desks. The openplan office like a cemetery and their smiles full of lives they reek envy and despair chatting out of their heads. The little boss propped in grey silhouette along the blind's strips. He toddles out assertive with lessons and speaks carefully and looks you straight in the eye his small brown and red eyes in his red and blue sick skin. His voice caked in smoke and the usual beer. His shakey voice anyway talks sentences. Where they taught him he goes up and down. He sits straight up in his chair. His face cracks open to a friend. His sentence grinds to a dead halt (silence) he looks you straight in the phone

---

She's bright as a button, old Marg, he says, impeccably even though a typist. There's no mistaking. She picks things up like that his textured pink shirt-sleeve zips the air. He looks benevolently down his nose.

They make conversation out of nothing. If you don't listen to the words, you can hear their voices stretch and whine a scale of boredom. He turns his attention to the woman like a microscope his words prattling and jilting his voice twinks her cheek. He pushes his pram of attention. The patronizing men move off in their quiet grey clothes their hushed voices. His pretty ribbon words she springs to catch his sweet knife she marks on her ribs, latches

The bland shopping centre heat slaps against your head, the flat blue cloudless sky hangs behind the square white outline of the complex. I walk around and around it, anything is better than the grey cowering air-conditioning. He waits in the lunch-room to expound his brains. I read the paper bent with my back to him, but he persists, baiting for war, defending America's 'democracy' at the drop of a crumb, his voice which had waited, ready to carp on, carps on softly, mildly, reasonably, carping on, as blood swills inside my head, his blue eyes picked in his red skin which had waited also to be paid attention like a receipt, to exist. I wrap up his cashed words in a mane of silence, his affected reasonable barbs reason their way into the back of my neck coming out of his mouth like a caption I read it and get fired that he interrupts for a start wanting to bridle me and to avert the cling between my eyes and the paper He hogs my last free minute and then takes you back like a patient guided gently into your personal jail for the rest of the afternoon at the staring clock and her terrified plastic tense coldness that I've given up on or kill Her voice bangling up and down in mindless rhythm behind sheds of work dumbly directing, not actually driving, beneath her and nothing I do pleases being out of line

Ms Princely continues her thick potted arguments and complaints through the trellis of files I move away from choked and christened with, her twice wife's mouth like a fish opening and shutting for air or steam as little discoloured pearly bubbles blurt in and out. Ms Valencia Ivory Psalter v.i.p.s around wagging her skirt eyelids over her dumbfound eyes Why do you always argue? she says, always arguing. You have no respect, she says, having no respect, as I wrap myself in arrogance like a stole To hate so vastly and imperiously is like a blessing I cleanse myself in I clock back to my desk like a throne, martyred and pinnacled on her hive of pettiness Look at my boys, harmlessly working away, she directs the two 30-yr-old clerks to file away her letters, husbands, face-packs, the articles on assertiveness-training for women that she henges around, solidifying with the other women, me for instance, only for a tableau to be looked at, a wall to be pillaged She treats the girls like tripe Here are two little nights out of the hundreds that are mine to delegate, she bodkins the extra dough to her chest, greed guttered on her stick tiara, she presses Jack and his endless performing dinner to the phone as he husbands to meet his meal at the platform to prick it home, a bit extra for your trip, two little gassed nights for you when I allow and dub thee, she nervily generously trolleys out to me I have a wirey taxless stressless job for you she rankles on as I stare at the pigeons on the balcony I swim the channel as she clusters to the point She gives it to me, to placate the cutlery of her papers, to dry them and dress them and wipe them I kneel on the floor in my arrow suit dusting up as her lion dollies charge anachronistically through the arena

———————————————

typist

Nobody wants to employ a typist who's older
than the supervisor because you lack
respect and are not scared and don't
have the right attitude and work
at your own pace because you know
about RSI and don't take on
administrative tasks because
you are paid shit to type
so that's all you'll do
and you roll your eyes
at superiors' mistakes
and bad handwriting
and keep an eye
on the clock and
won't stay late
and don't give
a fuck for
pretty dresses
and sucking up to the boss
and impressing with enthusiasm
and keeping the office neat and clean
just like home and putting up posters and
watering plants and going out of your way
and aiming high and offering to make tea
and completely revamping the office system
and clearing out all the files and remembering
people's birthdays and smiling and laughing all the time
like good office girls do and even if you're a
really good typist it's not good enough because
nobody wants to employ a typist older than the supervisor
because you KNOW TOO MUCH.

safer than sex

LAUREN WILLIAMS

I want a filing cabinet,
four drawers high in cool grey metal
Pot plant on top and a place
to rest my weary cheek
Label drawers carefully
Label files inside the drawers
Label folders inside the files
I will go to the stationery shop
and be stationary,
reverent in front of office supplies
Respectfully fondle tabs and stickers
Buy a black texta, write large
TO BE DONE / URGENT / TODAY
A B C D E F G
93 / 94 / 95 / 96
TAX / BILLS / BANKCARD RECEIPTS
A special file for love letters
Cabinet reshuffle when I'm bored
or look through Miscellaneous
More intelligent than spectacles
With a smooth slide of the drawers
I will dance with my square-shouldered friend
Analogue data base
An open and shut case.

footplate classics

Hey Ev
you're good at your job
I'd ask you to fire for me
anyday before the boys
BUT
do you really think
this is women's work?

I think lady firemen
should wear nice skirts
not overalls
they look so unfeminine
By the way
did you really hit a driver
over the head with a shifter
or is that just a rumour?

I know that you girls
can do the job
you've proved you're
better than the boys
BUT
I wouldn't let my
wife or daughter
become a train driver
ANYHOW
they wouldn't want to
cause they're
REAL WOMEN

EVELYN WILLIAMS

Thanks for firing
a tough shift
not exactly
what real women do
at 2am
dig blocked
sand boxes out
put sand on the rails
in front of a T class
struggling up Macedon
in heavy rain
do you really like
this work
OR
are you here
just to find
a husband?

An almost daily occurrence on walking
into South Dynon loco mealroom
Quiet fellows
no swearing
one of the girls
has just walked in
keep the language
clean
at 3am.

One morning
tired/frustrated/angry
I responded
I DON'T GIVE A FUCK
IF YOU SWEAR
result
immediate quiet
but for days/months
on my entering the mealroom
some boys voiced sentences
made solely of swear words.

Ev
is it true you're a leso
I've heard a rumour
all you girls are
you don't wear make up
you like getting your hands dirty
you want to drive trains
and you don't watch men
walking up station platform ramps
ALSO
I've heard when you
relieved at Dimboola
in the wheat season
that girl who shared your room
was your girlfriend
is that true
OR
were you really after Bernie
the locomotive assistant
they say you spent a lot
of time with him?

Great
I'm glad you're
firing for me
have you brought
the scones and cream
oh bad luck
well I guess
you'll make a decent
cup of tea
another cup I asked
after drinking it
he refrained
I don't blame him
the spoon stood
tall in the leaves.

Ev
you're a commie aren't you
not that I mind
BUT
some of the blokes
don't like pinkos
they say you came here
to cause trouble
to stir things up
not that I mind
mind you
you do a great job
on the footplate.

I reckon it's great
you girls are here
to teach the guys
a thing or two
I was talking
to my girlfriend
the other day
we reckon you lot
have footballs
it took me
a long while
to work
that one
out.

in search of princess panda

EVELYN

Do you know
about the little girl
who went in search
of a Princess?
Well, of course you don't
so I'll tell you . . . .

Once, a long time ago
at least twenty-five years ago
there was a dyke.

A dyke singing and playing a guitola; you know, a four string instrument, like a guitar but smaller. Playing a guitola on the Happpy Hammond show. Do you remember the Happy Hammond show? Princess Panda was on it. She used to dress up like a real Princess: long net dresses, high-heels and make up. She was the doll. And Joffa Boy was on it. Do you remember his shout: 'How dee do dee Boys and Girls.' And we kids were meant to yell back from home: 'How dee do dee Joffa Boy.' He was the 'Funny Man' but he wasn't very funny. Happy Hammond was the compere, he wore the loud checked jacket and hat. You remember it now, don't you?

Well, back to the dyke. In reality heaps of dykes have been on the Happy Hammond show but I know this one was for sure. She was one of the 'Home Kids'. Happy Hammond had a series of special segments - you probably don't remember them - they weren't that eventful. Kids from different homes around Victoria went into Channel 9, went onto the set and performed for the 'better off kids at home'. This dyke came from Kardinia children's home in Geelong. It was run by the Salvos.

Performing was not new to her. Like circus clowns, kids in homes were called on to show everybody that they were looked after, dressed OK, that they were 'loved'. Parents everywhere also used Home Kids to threaten their own offspring, saying 'if you don't behave I'll send *you* to a home!'

But this dyke thought this was special; hadn't seen a T.V. studio before, hadn't seen Princess Panda close up, or in colour. She was really excited. The kids from the home were dressed in their best white dresses, hair done just so with Brylcream and bows. They waited in a small room; all nervous, chatting incessantly. They weren't able to see the show, just had to wait for someone to tell them when it was time.

Well, someone finally came, took them into a studio and showed them where to stand. Lots of noise all around but no Princess Panda, no Happy Hammond, or the dreaded Joffa Boy. They were told to start. The dyke was smiling and jiggling and moving around to the music. They played 'Don't fence me in', which seems a bit ironic now: 'Give me land lots of land and the starry skies above/ Don't fence me in.' But then this dyke was performing, doing what she was conditioned to do. Performing with a smile showing the world what they wanted to see. Home Kids were really happy.

Afterwards she thought she'd been conned. Never saw any of the show and couldn't even see the kids in the audience. Didn't see Princess Panda to see if she was for real. Why did they dress her like that anyway? All she'd seen was a camera; performing for a camera. Adults at the home saw them and said they were great.

They especially liked my smile.

I almost felt cheated all over again.
But this time I had one up on them.

Amidst all
that smiling
and jiggling
piss
was trickling
down my legs
onto my
white socks
over my
black shoes
to the floor
a yellow puddle
forming at my feet.

After strumming the last chord, with my head held high, this dyke
walked out of that studio smiling.

sister jessie

MARY BASTABLE

A GLUED-ON DEER DRANK from a bright blue painted river in a tiny rural scene above our mantelpiece. Then it was overlaid by the new Kingdom calender, by its vivid colours. The calender showed us the smooth, tanned legs and thick Brylcreem-ed hair of a shepherd. Like one of the Hollywood actors in *Photoplay* magazine. Angled to a crook, he smiled down on sheep and lambs with an eye to the camera. The landscape may have been a land from the Bible, or the west coast of Scotland. Sinuous red letters traced the text: 'And I will give you shepherds in agreement with my heart, and they will certainly feed you with knowledge and insight' (Jeremiah 3:15).

The Kingdom calender dominated our living room. It was incidental here on Jessie's picture rail. This was a big house. Used rooms. Open doors. Jessie's front room was a lounge. A large, comfortable space with sunshine walls. Sparsely furnished; always fresh flowers. And a sparkling baby grand.

My shoes were spit-and-polished. At each step toward the sofa they sank into the carpet's dark roses. Snakeskin stilettos tiptoed to a matching grey velvet armchair. Jessie sailed away to make tea. An undertone urged: 'Tidy your skirt up, love and get that fringe back out of your eyes, do . . . .'

Jessie stood in for Sister Doris in providing musical accompaniment for the songs at our Kingdom Hall meetings. We met three times each week. On Tuesdays there was the Bible book study group at someone's home. But on Thursday nights and Sunday afternoons we met at the Kingdom Hall. We rented the dance hall behind the Fellowship Inn pub at Bellingham. It was Henry Cooper's pub; boxer, mate of the Krays. He lived there, and would lean out of the upstairs window and wave to us after the meeting on Sunday . . . .

The Fellowship Inn's piano wasn't up to much. Doris played with flamboyant insistence. It was different for Jessie. Her touch was gentle, her baby fingers wanting to caress the keys. She would do her duty at the Congregation Servant's request, but her suede kitten heels carried her to the piano reluctantly. Jehovah loved Jessie, my mother knew, because she was like the brother in the Bible who said he wouldn't help with the harvest but did. Doris, on the other hand, was seen as having to wrestle with a tendency towards arrogance. Her dramatic presentation of Song 73, for example, incorporated *her own* twirly bits.

So, in a way my Mum was the bearer of a gift of recognition from the Lord by bringing me to Jessie for counselling. So Jessie might know that the Lord saw fit to use her as his vessel, and count herself a fellow Counsellor with Sister Mary who was stumped by this one . . . .

Jessie carried in delicate tea things whose use was clearly nothing out of the ordinary. I had extra milk and sugar. Big Mary had it strong, milk-no-sugar, and stuck out her little finger to raise her spirits. She fidgeted uncomfortably on the edge of her chair. Jessie placed herself against the piano, resting one elbow on its curve. A high-quality crimplene dress stretched across her well-corseted breasts made an impressive monobosom. You could tell high-quality Crimplene; its colours were muted, like 'art', and its patterns were of rich embossed flowers. These flowers were roses, in tones of beige and grey.

I could tell that Sister Jessie didn't find this easy, was uncomfortable, shifting from one beige leather court shoe to the other. We established that the problem was my lack of faith. Everlasting Life on a paradise earth was God's promised reward for obedience and faithful evangelising but I did not want to live forever. The global battle which was to herald the New System disturbed me: every carnage must involve some error. And I liked sinners.

According to Scripture I'd be safe through the Battle; I was an obedient nine year old. There was every prophetic indication that it would all be over before I reached an age where I could be held responsible. My mother's salvation would cover me. But I knew that I was already responsible: 'So if any of you is lacking in wisdom, let him keep on asking God, for he gives generously to all and without reproaching; and it will be given him. But let him keep on asking in faith, not doubting at all, for he who doubts is like a wave of the sea driven by the wind and blown about' (James 1:5,6). I knew myself to be that faithless man; I just didn't know what I could do about it. I prayed and prayed but I couldn't want what was promised.

'You don't want to die, do you love?'
'No... but....'
'Then you want to live for ever.'

It was a problem of desire. I wanted Big Mary's love and approval but I needed to get my 'thinking straight with the Lord'. I wanted Sister Jessie's counselling to work. When Mother left the room to wash up the tea things, Jessie sat beside me on the sofa and folded me into her huge bosom. Her baby fingers, with buffed nails of translucent pink, cradled my forearm. She smelled of fresh roses and her string of fine pearls trickled into my mouth as she hugged me. I wanted to relax into the cuddle, or for both of us to cry.... 'If you can carry on being obedient to Jehovah and being a good girl, I'm sure the faith will come, and it will make your mother so happy,' she whispered. I inhaled her worried smile. 'Can I tell your Mum you'll try to do that? And you can come and talk to me whenever you want to.'

When my mother returned, Jessie stood by the piano again and presented my undertaking and her offer. Mother was both humble and vindicated; I knew the look. She suggested that we 'say thank you to Jehovah', and led a brief communique before we started the long walk home.

Later, Jessie would often ask how things went with me. My answers were hopeful, optimistic; the gaze was distant. I'd taken my part in a story where problems of belief and desire had no place. Their absence, the silence, served the purpose of faith for a while.

bloody marys

Mary, Mary quite contrary
How does your garden grow?
With silver bells and cockle shells
And pretty maids all in a row.

MAGDALENE WAS BORN IN THE foyer of a hospital. She couldn't wait to get out, embrace herself and embark upon a journey worthy of her birth. Magdalene already had a brother when she was born, but soon brought him into line. He could read, ride a bicycle, but she caught up fast. The trouble was, with all this catching up, Magdalene lost sight of why she was doing it. He was 'doing it' because it addressed him, it suited him, was tailored for him. She did it because she wanted the same for herself, but it was never quite the same. It was easy, the school-work, but she knew or guessed that there were other things she was learning; things that were directed at her, that weren't as straightforward. She learnt secrecy and watching.

The blackboard principle tells us what we know is already known. Is the innocence of youth some self-fulfilling prophecy, pre-written (or at least transferred through archetypes), chalked up by those written themselves?

Mary was not quite sure who owned what. She knew that what belonged to her was a type of maintenance job; a job involving the upkeep of her body and mind. First she had thought that she belonged to her family. That was certainly true for a while, but as her life went on her world got bigger, as did her family, and things became a little less clear.

Mary learnt about sex early on in high school from her friends. At first it was difficult to piece this new knowledge (this real knowledge) in with what she'd acquired from her fairy-tale books, but facts never really had much to do with truths so the incompatibility was never more than a fact. Sizzle, sizzle went her brain cells as she walked carefully around the rocks, the cliff looming nearer. She could leap off into the hands of romantic love - she wondered why she hadn't thought of it before - but then again nothing is original, is it? At least the rocks were solid.

Magdalene sat in the nude in the bathroom feeling her insides draw themselves together and apart. It was like a tearing sensation: fishhooks attached to her uterus, pulling down, ripping to get out. How little blood did get out though. She'd expected the bleeding to be more somehow, like the amount of piss that comes out when the bladder is distended with pain. But no, it wasn't as satisfying as that. And there were chewy bits besides.

Magdalene decided to do something with it. She collected some butchers' paper and sat down on it, pressing her cunt onto the off-white surface. A blob of red came out, a mixture of thick and thin which absorbed into the paper. She splattered it this way and that with her hands inscribing the paper and her body at once. Magdalene imagined the 'Shroud of Turin' . . . art as religion, body as art, her biology as destiny, as plagiarism.

I'm a virgin, thought Mary, 'touched for the very first time . . . .' Madonna wasn't really one of her favourites. She couldn't imagine having sex with her; she'd know too much. But then again she couldn't imagine actually having sex with anyone. She just thought about it. Mary knew she was ripening, if ripening was the right word for it. Mary had a friend at school, Magdalene, and she sure as hell hoped she wouldn't ripen like that. Mary's sense of belonging had been replaced by a sense of ownership. Mary knew she belonged to her father. Her mother belonged to her father. She knew, now that she was developing, that she'd better be careful with her father's property.

It was one week until Mary's fifteenth birthday. Mary felt inclined to tell everyone to fuck off. She felt like a stuck pig. Her dress, clearly in league against her, told her she looked like one too. Her body ached towards something she couldn't define. Her body buzzed alarmingly. Mary's mother said, 'That's the clock dear, you'll be late for school,' and Mary clenched her fist, hating. This feeling was to continue regularly, lasting about a week, every month for years.

Mary sat on the bathroom floor, contradiction rising up through her throat, 'Its the scream that comes from nowhere that frightens me. The scream that says here I am. To be nowhere is to be that which is unspeakable. How much to scream is a question of taste. How loud, how long, low, high, and for what. Do not consider the scream which says: Do Not Continue.'

Mary's first period had come. It was foul and smelly, but at least she was a woman now. Great delight was to be taken in spending the money she received from her weekend job on feminine deodorants. Not so much fun purchasing the sanitary napkins, but you've got to take the crunchy with the smooth.

Although she'd worked out how to buy several packets of napkins at once from the man in the chemist - to save half the humiliation and embarrassment - Mary was not so organised in the disposal department. Dread and an incapacity for action overtook her as she considered the alternatives. Someone might see them if she put them in the kitchen-tidy, and she was sure that the title 'sanitary' was not a descriptive term. Mary sat in her room staring indirectly at the soiled napkins of the past few days, her mind blank. An irresistible urge overtook her. She grabbed one of the wretched things and threw it out the window.

It was some time before Mary was able to summon up the courage to look out and see where the napkin had got to. The unspeakable had happened; there it was, lodged quite firmly in the upper branches of a tree. Worse still, this same tree was the one that shaded the living-room downstairs. Panic struck. Mary looked desperately around her room, her eyes catching on a bag of marbles. Her attempts were in vain. The bag got smaller, the rag loomed redder. The curse, I curse it all, then I forget. (Taboo as embarrassment.)

Mary's attention turned to the remaining evidence. She sat on the edge of her bed calmly tearing pages from her mother's *Family Circle*. Wrapping each bloodied napkin neatly, she gathered them up, five in all, and placed them carefully in the top drawer of her duchesse, next to her socks and underpants. Satisfied, she shut it firmly, triumphantly. The next day, when Mary returned home from school, she saw her mother going indoors with a plastic bag and a broom handle. Mary's flag had gone. Her top drawer continued to grow in its contents for the next seven months. Biological process as social process.

School was over, finally. The stifling irrelevance of it all. Magdalene packed her bags and, smiling quietly to herself, laid her first true artworks onto the floor. The paper had become yellowed with age and the blood a delicious brown-black. Her insides throbbed with intense pleasure as she carefully folded the sacred items and filed them in the bin. Art as wishful thinking. Magdalene was heading off to the city, to art school.

Her arrival was not less than her coming, and Magdalene soon settled into her new life with Joy. Life is paradox and contradiction is a process. Magdalene cut her hair, donned Doc Martens and slipped into a life of pseudo-bohemia.

One Friday afternoon, Magdalene took her usual detour via Joy's workplace and loitered next to the vitamin-and-minerals section, checking the last customers out as Joy shut up shop. One was a short man with a round bald pate purchasing dental floss and a bottle of Grecian 2000. The other looked very familiar but Magdalene had difficulty placing her.

Mary couldn't help smiling, Magdalene had always had that effect on her.

'Let's go to the 'Half Moon', ok?' said Joy.

On the way, Magdalene said wait a sec, and left Mary and Joy chatting on the footpath. She disappeared through the golden arches of McDonalds.

Magdalene made a b-line for the toilets, reluctantly negotiating a table with six or seven skate-bored boys. They leered, 'Cop a load of that!'

'Hey you can't go in there, you're no lady,' one of them quipped. Ha, ha. The others were quick to join in.

'Fucking leso.'

'Bull-dyke slut.'

'What is it?'

'Show us ya tits.'

Once inside the cubicle, Magdalene calmed down enough to do a quick perusal of the graffiti offerings. Nothing worthwhile . . . oh well.

Just in time, Magdalene thought to herself as she removed a sodden, dripping sea-sponge from between her legs. Sponges always made her think of mermaids and luscious fishy things. This feeling of solidarity gave her courage. She deftly inserted a new sponge - Magdalene always carried a spare - and held the full one warmly in her half closed hand. Her eyes were caught by 'war is menstruation envy' as she headed for the sink, and a smile struck her face as she went back through the cafeteria towards the boys.

'Eat your hearts out, fellas,' she said calmly, surprised at herself, as she let the blood-soaked sponge drop onto the middle of their table, splattering blood oozing onto their Big Macs. They didn't move. Their mouths gaped. Their eyes stared incomprehensively, stunned. It seemed like a lifetime. Magdalene strode confidently through the chaos and out to where Mary and Joy were waiting.

untitled

VICKI PINGLE

Even though her body was covered

in lacerations
red, clotty furrows

with tatty flesh

edges

she still

yearned to have every hole
filled

fucked

full
over, above, too much beyond

thinking

always before the event
that

it would plug up the void
but each time

lying spent
she chilled as her sweat dried

the emptiness would come back

creeping at first
hardly detectable
growing nevertheless.

coping

Milk glugs forth from the hole in my breast,
thick and creamy with a slight tinge of red.
That hole used to be my nipple,
quite firmly attached to my left lump.

That nipple now lies on the floor,
next to your underpants,
ripped clean off like a boot.
You spat it over that way 20 minutes ago.
I heard it land after it hit the wall,
then moaned rather loudly.

Did you notice
all the white stuff smeared between us?
I don't think you did
even though the entire mattress was wet.
You slept alright.
You snored and thumped your arm across my ebbing breast
at five past three.

I got up before you,
sewed myself back together
with wrong colour cotton,
put on a bra
and made breakfast.

VICKI PINGLE

outside it snows

JYANNI STEFFENSEN

WHAT IS INVOLVED IN THE discovery of the 'true story' within or behind the events that come to us in the chaotic form of 'historical records'? What wish is enacted, what desire is gratified, by the fantasy that real events are properly represented when they can be shown to display the formal coherency of a story? In the enigma of this wish, this desire, we catch a glimpse of the cultural function of narrativising discourse.

The historian's desire for a moral order.

She cannot always be indifferent. Her lover has a ruby in her navel and cornflakes in her hair. She has cruising on her mind.
   Pardon me, I must be going.
   Very well, I shall begin again.
   Everyone lives in a city called THE CAPITAL. The action takes place in the Sheraton Hotel in Sofia between 8.25pm and 5am. It is winter. Outside it snows. Sofia has long black hair, curled, and extraordinarily large eyes.
   Two women board a train. Their destination is unclear. Unethical and undetermined. They exchange briefcases. This is the Law of Exchange. Or the Law of Briefcases. She stares at her lover's desk. It lies unwritten on the page.

Can we imagine, or should we, a position that speaks in tropes and walks in sensible shoes. In other words — for the moment, I am not fucking. I am talking to you. Well, I can have the same satisfaction as if I were fucking. That's what it means. Indeed, it raises the question of whether in fact I am not fucking at this moment. There can be satisfaction, in other words, at giving up satisfaction. Desire moves around.

Now you see us . . . .
Now you don't.

Second Tableau.
Describes scenes in which two women figure. You and your lover embrace naked in a room. Your lover enters the scene and after, you leave and disappear.

Sixth Tableau.
Describes you and your lover fucking on a table. Outside the window are described a multiplicity of scenes of the world. There is a major category error at the core of metaphysics.

I had this dream. I dreamed I was walking with friends. I saw a black cat and I picked it up and I ate it. The drive is indifferent to its object. Desire is indifferent to its object . . . . Desire, like power, inscribes its subject(s). This is a game of seduction.

An actress who looks exactly like Greta Garbo will board the train. In fourteen minutes time. She will be smoking a small cigar. She will know you by the colour of your eyes. She will leave the train before it reaches its destination. She will leave another in its place.

A bisexual sadomasochist has no shadow. A glitter in the darkness. The cruelty is in the text for anyone to read. A bomb explodes (unexpectedly) in the wrong place. The film just keeps flickering in a darkened cinema. The audience remains attentively silent. She suddenly remembers *Another Way*. A doomed love affair. Between two women journalists. In Hungary. During a politically volatile period. Someone quotes its 'pure eroticism'. The time is 1956.

The Scene. A hotel room. Somewhere. Outside, it snows. On the sixth floor it is quiet and cool. The window overlooks a swimming pool on

the roof of another building. Another hotel perhaps. It is empty. The pool, that is. It has water but no one swims in it.
What is it then to say 'the pool is empty'?

Scene One. Two women are in the room. One of them stands by the window looking out. She smokes a cigarette (lazily). The other is sitting on the bed. She adjusts her stockings. The other turns. Looks at her.

Theory is first defined as a reading. Even when you stuff the mouth – the mouth that opens in the register of the drive – it is not the food that satisfies it, it is, as one says, the pleasure of the mouth . . . it is obvious that it is not a question of food, nor the echo of food, nor the memory of food but of something which is called the breast. The pleasure moves around tricking objects.

Her lover turns. Warm from sleep. Her body is covered in sweat. She smells of heat and fucking. Her eyes are transparent. She stretches. Slides her body over the sheets. Her lips brush her lover's shoulder. Scenes. The street is silent. Her cunt hovers ambivalently between pleasure and pain. I knew you would say that.

She stumbles by chance on a fragment of a photograph. In the gutter. The train thunders toward Vers-Roissy.

Imagine a woman who steals letters.
Imagine a woman who exposes herself.

At 8pm precisely the performance will begin. The door will be locked. No one will enter after 8.02.

A train pulls into a station. A woman gets off. Walks slowly and deliberately amongst hurrying people. The same languid movement. A man turns his head. Watches her. She does not alter her pace. Looks neither right or left. She crosses the square. Enters a hotel. He follows her. When he reaches the lobby she has disappeared.

I plot and stalk her with arousing cunning . . . planning strategy. To get her into bed. Tied up, strapped down. Her slender white body pegged out for my delight. Her legs tied apart. She can't move. Is at my mercy. My control. Her lovely black curly-haired cunt. Those wide black eyes. Sadistic lust. I pinch her rose-pink nipples. They stand up. Erect.

'I'm glad you are in such good humour,' said the painter, 'but your face has lost the expression which I need for my picture.'

'The expression which you need for your picture,' she replied, smiling. 'Wait a moment.'

She rose and dealt me a blow with the whip. The painter looked at her with stupefaction, and a childlike surprise showed on his face, mingled with disgust and admiration.

Words pile up. In the night she is restless. The TV does not comfort her. She prowls. Words do not console her. Images haunt her. A TV monitor is strapped to the window. The text is on the screen.

What he is trying to see, make no mistake, is the object as absence. What the voyeur is looking for and finds is merely a shadow, a shadow behind the curtain. There she will phantasise anything, the most beautiful of women, for instance, even if on the other side there is only *objét petit a*. What one looks at is what cannot be seen. It is located somewhere between the eye and the gaze.

Her lover turns. Presses her knee gently between her legs. They part. Touch here. Caress this spot. & here. She has a number tattooed on the nape of her neck. Under the skin. Eat my skull eat my bones suck out my brains rip out my spine. Serenity becomes her. She is a wicked woman. A fatal femme. She always seems to be *noir* lit. Someone is watching this scene.

A reception. Outside it snows. Everything seems muted. A low hum. Two women enter, wearing black trench coats and hats. They look at art work for a while. They walk up behind a well dressed man. Take his arms, one on either side and continue out the door, down the steps and into a waiting car.

The man in the metro is the lover of the man in the apartment opposite her hotel. His window has no blinds. He will be carrying a notebook.

You think desire. It is all the more intense. Your desire for her body.

The phone rings. It is the man from the apartment opposite her hotel. He says I am calling from New York. She can see his mouth moving.

Her eyes smile. My cunt throbs. I run the tip of the whip over her skin. Down her belly and the inside of her thigh. Push it up against her clit and rub it back and forth. Stroking lightly. Her cunt floods. Her back arches. Strains against the bonds. I smack her thigh. A bright red welt appears. Her eyes smart.

Two women board a train. One of them pulls the stop cord. Between stations. She leaves the train. In the middle of a desert. She crosses the border. At night. She remains distant impassive ironical and watching. Every word every image is leased and mortgaged.

Is not this mouth what might be called a mouth in the form of an arrow. A mouth kissing itself. The tension is always loop-shaped. 'I look', 'I am looked at', 'I look at myself'.

The younger sister has written: 'When I'm dead place a stone on my face so I won't haunt you. When I'm dead cut off one of my hands and bury it at the crossroads so I won't rise again and torment you. I've killed myself against you. You are the target of my death therefore protect yourself against me.'

The writer says not wanting success could be a sign of life. She says not if you die of it. Her lover is the object. Of her desire. The object of writing.

While whipping me, Maria's face acquired more and more of the cruel, contemptuous character that so haunts and intoxicates me.

'Is this the expression you need for your picture?' she asked. The painter lowered his look in confusion before the cold ray of her eye.

'It is the expression – ' he stammered, 'but I can't paint now – '

'What?' said Maria, scornfully. 'Perhaps I can help you?'

'Yes – ' cried the painter, as if taken by madness. 'Whip me too!'

'Oh! With pleasure,' she replied, shrugging her shoulders.

'But if I am to whip you, I want to do it in sober earnest.'

'Whip me to death,' cried the painter.

Are you sure of that?

This is a three-dimensional question. Here I would like to make a distinction between the motive and the object of desire. The motive is roots, flesh and skin. It is incontournable. It is carnal knowledge. All good writers have a strong motive. Dreams are three-dimensional but we forget about *them*.

The Beautiful Bald Blond Woman is writing.

She begins . . . .

I was delivering a seminar paper on lesbian poetics. Afterwards, a man approached me and engaged me in a conversation about my work. He was a stranger, although not altogether unknown to me. I was intrigued, a little, as to why he did this as he did not know me and he, as it turned out, was not a known homosexual.

She moves her hand across her lover's belly. Down into the soft blond hair. She curls it gently around her fingers. Pulls up abruptly. Her lover grins. Her eyes smart. She moves her fingers further. Touches the electric space to the left of her lover's clit. Her legs spasm. Big belly muscles contract. Relax. Her fingers snake the join of thigh and cunt. She will pretend to be asleep. Without meaning (to). She pulls her lover's body into her own. A line dissecting armpit and breast.

Scene 4: Inside the hotel room. The two women in black trench coats enter with the well dressed man – a diplomat, a cultural attaché? In the room are a spectacular looking woman, the one from the train station scene, and an angelic blond young man. They drink champagne. Talk and laugh softly. They appear indifferent to the presence of the women and the diplomat.

The first scene lends itself to a number of floral associations. Artichokes, for example. The sexual relation is thus not a relation between two subjects, but rather between five things – the Other, the subject, the other, the phantasm of the other desired by the subject, and the phantasm of the subject desired by the other.

She tongues the swollen pink clit. Wraps her mouth around it. Works it between her teeth. Her fingers sneak up behind. Into her delicious little arsehole. She wriggles them inside. Two then three. Inching her way up. Sofia grunts softly. Rolls over. Side-up. Her hair is red. Red and curly. Her teeth are white. Thick and white. She smiles. Her mouth is thick and broad. She has a diamond in her nose. Her eyes are blue. Or brown. Her hair curls down her back. Almost to her waist.

Her voice is distant. A glitter in the darkness. In the blackness it

snows. By the telephone is a written message. An adult movie in your room. Call the desk. They will charge you. The bodies wait, entangled in the lines. There is nothing on the screen but snow.
Are there any further questions? The text ends.

An actress looking exactly like Greta Garbo will enter from off-screen. In forty minutes. She will sit at a desk and clean her gun. She will straighten the seams of her stockings and leave the room. She will lock the door behind her. She will walk down a long hallway.

Her lover leaves the scene. She turns the page. She is dismantled.

Finally, she seemed tired. She tossed the whip aside, stretched out on the ottoman, and rang.

The woman in black entered.

'Untie him!' As they loosened the ropes, I fell to the floor like a lump of wood. The women in black grinned, showing their white teeth. 'Untie the rope around his feet.'

They did it, but I was unable to rise.

'Come over here.'

I approached the beautiful woman. Never did she seem more seductive to me than today in spite of all her cruelty and contempt.

'One step further,' Maria commanded. 'Now kneel down, and kiss my foot.'

You ought to be like this. I warm myself by warming myself is a reference to the body as body — I feel that sensation of warmth which, from some point inside me, is diffused and locates me as body. Whereas in the 'I see myself seeing myself', there is no such sensation of being absorbed by vision. Where are you? I know where I am, but I do not feel as though I am at the spot where I find myself.

The receiver is glued to her ear. She breathes into the other one. I want 14 strand high voltage wire. Give it to me now. She blows into her nostril. She has a theory of fucking and flying.

Fist-fucked to heaven.

A train pulls into a station (as in Scene #2). The Beautiful Woman gets off as before. A man watches her from behind a newspaper. He folds it carefully and follows her. She crosses the square to the university and disappears. To put it another way: the option left to me was to have a

fling with the philosophers, which is easier said than done....
   Two women steal luggage. From Lost Property. At the terminal. There are railway cars full of suitcases. The man who interprets the dream is a psychiatrist. The woman he interprets for has given him her suitcase. Two women steal it back. It contains pages of a story about two women who steal luggage. The psychiatrist is surprised. The woman who dreamed her suitcase was stolen is not.
   The woman at the window idly picks up a pair of binoculars. She watches a man in the apartment opposite the hotel window. Another man enters the apartment, takes off his coat, hangs it up and enters the room where the other man is seated at a desk talking on the phone. He is similar. Not similar to something, but just similar....

Who are these characters? What are they doing here? On this page. Wild thoughts in another direction. Stinking hot. Wasted days. Outside it snows...

She carves words into her lover's belly. Blood stains the sheets. Drips onto the carpet. She carves words into her lover's brain. Cells divide and multiply. Split and fuse.
   Desire dissolves.
   A woman's hand reaches over and unsnaps a stocking from a garter belt. Rolls it down and slides her hand inside a creamy white thigh.
   She pushes through the turnstile. At the train station. Hurtles down two escalators. Onto the platform. In one movement. She smokes her second last cigarette.
   'May I really whip him?' he asked.
   'Do with him what you please,' replied Maria.
   'Beast!' I shouted, utterly revolted.
   He fixed his cold look upon me and tried out the whip. His muscles swelled when he drew back his arms and made the whip hiss through the air.
   One can have a body that does not necessarily co-incide with the actuality of one's anatomy – a shadow body. Some other body. A body that no one can see. No body.
      The man with the newspaper is watching the entrance to the university. The woman comes out. He follows her. She passes the

hotel. Another woman comes out of the hotel and follows the man. She takes his photograph. It is not a photograph of the body, but a map of the degrees of erotogenicity on its surface. An image of its significance.

Scene #1.
Two women are lying naked. On a bed. In a hotel room. One of them gets up. Puts on a black dress. She picks up a dossier puts it in a briefcase and leaves the room. The other woman wakes up. Gets up. Puts on black pants and sweater. She puts some items in a briefcase and leaves. Locking the door behind her. A man wearing a white hat watches them.

'It is the expression – ' he stammered.

'What?' said Maria scornfully. 'Perhaps I can help you?'

This theory comes as a complete shock to Freud. He is dumbfounded.

Interior. The hotel room. Champagne glasses. The diplomat and the angelic young man are kissing. The women have disappeared. Slowly they begin to undress each other.

She lies. She leaves. No clues.

'Will you let me tie you?' she asked, smiling.

'Yes – ' he moaned.

Maria left the room for a moment, and returned with ropes.

'Well – are you still brave enough to put yourself into the power of Ms X., the beautiful despot, for better or worse?' she began ironically.

'Yes, tie me,' the painter replied dully.

Maria tied his hands behind his back, drew a rope through his arms and a second one around his body, and fettered him to the crossbars of the window. Then she rolled back her fur sleeve, seized the whip, and stepped in front of him.

Her lover leaps from the train. Hits the ground running. Crosses the border. She translates documents into other languages. She masquerades. She leaves. No trace. The Government destabilises. The police are anxious.

The phone rings. It is the man from the apartment opposite her hotel. He writes stories. His are about two women in a hotel room opposite his apartment.

The Beautiful Woman is addressing a class of students in a lecture theatre. She shows slides of the two men fucking in the hotel room. The man with the newspaper enters at the back of the room.

'I even remember something you said, which I couldn't explain to myself,' replied Leila. 'You made me lean over the water, and you said, 'Look at yourself. See how beautiful you are.' I replied that I was less so than you. 'Oh, but you are more beautiful,' she said. 'You look like a man'.'

She receives an invitation. 'We would be pleased if you could join us for this occasion.'
Thursday 6pm 28 September, 1990.
The Minister will be there. The Minister of Images.
The diplomat lies naked on the bed in the hotel room. He is alone. Slowly smoking a small cigar.
'Lead him to the bath,' Maria commanded, while she herself hurried away.
She ascends a Grand Staircase. In disguise. The Minister for Words is confused. She treads on his foot. You shouldn't make jokes if it makes you unhappy said Isabella. She has a fetish for Polystyrene Cups and Plastic Forks.

The Beautiful Woman is seated at a cafe reading and sipping coffee. The man with the newspaper approaches her. She looks up, curiously. He speaks to her briefly. She smiles, but shakes her head. He leaves. She is joined by the woman who has been photographing the man. They embrace. Kiss passionately. Laugh. The Beautiful Woman collects her papers. They leave. The man watches them from across the street.

A few moments passed and Maria arrived, dressed in nothing but the sable fur, with the whip in her hand. She descended the stairs and stretched out on the velvet cushions as on the former occasion. I lay at her feet, and she placed her foot upon me as her right hand played with the whip.

She enters the scene of narration in order to interrupt it. Authority here is a fiction. It can claim only the credit due the speculations of a reader.

In which language would she speak? The principles of lust are burned in the mind.

A taste for silk and fur. Certainly not fur. All those dead animals. I can never stroke a wild animal. It would bite my hand off. Leather, maybe. Certainly it would be a fetish suitable. Soft leather like fine gloves. So unsound to have a fetish for fur. Perhaps velvet is O.K. How many velvets died …? Etc. Certainly Leopold would be distressed at the thought. Suffer agonies in fact. Weep?

She said, for example, fetishism is the only perversion for which there is no corresponding neurosis. The female fetishist can see both the rabbit and the duck at the same time. Or one might say that the fetish is the negation of time insofar as it attempts to defer the arrival of death. A fetish is a fantasy of unity. Death is the fantasy in ruins, or, as someone said, the conquest of time.

She rolls a cigarette. Casually. Saunters out of town. Squints.

Scene 13. Interior. The hotel room. The two women in black enter with the diplomat. They undress him and tie him with silk ropes. The Beautiful Woman caresses his body then fist fucks him. He is excited. The two women and the blond young man drink champagne on the balcony.

The scene had a grim attraction for me, which I cannot describe. I felt my heart skip a beat when, with a smile, she drew back her arm for the first blow, and the whip hissed through the air. He winced slightly. Then she let blow after blow rain upon him, with her mouth half-opened and her teeth flashing between her red lips, until finally he seemed to ask for mercy with his piteous blue eyes. It was indescribable.

However these energies can also stagnate or drive you crazy if they don't meet their object of desire or organize in such a way that they can at least figure out their object of desire. Energy too intense makes noise instead of meaning. Digging in that field can be a mental health hazard for a woman. If the object isn't there nothing happens except sweat.

She cannot always be indifferent. Her lover has a ruby in her navel and cornflakes in her hair. She has cruising on her mind.

The man with the newspaper follows the Beautiful Woman into the hotel lobby. Fog drifts in from the street. He walks down a long carpeted hallway. Which door? He sees one slightly ajar. He opens it. Two women are rapt in each other's arms. Oblivious to his entrance. He cannot close the door. He is caught in their desire. For each other.

He is a journalist.

Elle a chaud au cul . . . and 'I' am in a/my body .

Everyone in the photograph looks so much like themselves. Just like themselves.

the prowler

MARION CAMPBELL

I AM A LITTLE GIRL and there's always a prowler outside my picture window. The prowler watches me watch. I paint what I want to watch in my picture window. Sometimes I paint the prowler myself. The prowler looks like me in some of these pictures. But I'm stuck in my spot and the prowler prowls. The prowler is sniggering in the gallery where I show my paintings. The prowler is the marauder in the margins of anything I write. The prowler says: *Arrest that signifier! See, this is what she means — if she's writing for anyone but her own onanistic circle* . . . . In his column the prowler calls me postmodern, postfeminist, posturing, agit-propagandist . . . . I check this in the mirror; the prowler is right. The prowler is my right hand. The prowler says: What are you looking at, girl? Wouldn't you like one too? This is what the little girl wants. The prowler says: I'll be your framer if you'll stay behind that picture window. Sometimes the prowler is God. Sometimes he is my dead father, the voice of the living women I want to please. The prowler's feverishly flicking eye and side shuffle are my own imposture returning in the dark. I write sometimes like a straight guy. What I dredge up in drag mode, you'd be surprised. The prowler returns to haunt me. The prowler's an old hand at cross-dressing. He finds me out when I sneak into his baggy pants, iron-shiny serge, low at the crotch, his twisted belt. The prowler is the paradigm policeman. He whispers at my ear: They'll say you're mad, self-indulgent, illiterate, ungrammatical, see how your rebel words clot with your fear. You'll never have the guts to be lawless like me, to be a real iconoclast; that means image-breaker, sweetheart.

I'm trained to think with a simulated alien brain. I'm in constant dialogue with it. I make a nice couple; I make a nuclear family all by myself. The prowler says: You will never paint your big fat inside-out sexual appetite because you're a goody-two-shoes. Obedience gives style and panache to your revolts. Kick a door open, you'd make sure your foot described an arabesque. The prowler incites and rebukes. The prowler wrote this on his visiting card.

the room

JORDIE ALBISTON

i am a woman locked in a
room in a house in a
suburb/you could call me

some kind of princess
though the only spinning
done is in my head/this is

my industry/i twirl a
gold thread of my own/i am
seated/back against door

awkward lotus/i work for
the good of the kingdom
look/the tapestries are torn

from the walls/they lie in
heaps/little piles of ash/i
have cut them to bits/i

have toiled for an age/i
have had to destroy those
centre spreads/see on the

floor/an eye/a fringe/a
slice of breast/my sour
flesh/your goddess

is chopped to pieces/she
is stacked on the floor
by my left knee/your queen

is in tatters though your
madwoman is quite intact/it
is you who have divided

me/made me white as virgin
black as whore/golden as any
good mother/it is over

it is enough/i have forged
my own knife/any myth
pale offering/i will shred

watch out/i am weaving a key
on my quivering loom/i know
my way out/i have measured

the depth of this tower/this
dungeon/my room/i will burst free
no phoenix/no dragon/but me

rape scene

it was the same act/old re-run
a little boring to the viewer perhaps
even the hero stifles a yawn   but
it was my first time/opening night
i could barely stammer my lines

the stage was set: suburban night naked
woman in bed man forces lock children
shift in sleep   i heard the cue
pretended to dream
the script called for sweat   i sweated

my doorway filled with shape/just like i knew
it would be   i watched the shape
circle/unzip/just like i thought
it would be   and you know and you
know when he breathed my air and strode

my bed bruised my flesh my silence my
home   my mind   just went   blank
stage-fright
i forgot   the lot   oh what
what did i say on the news in the paper the

report   did i scream yell weep submit did i
survive   oh susannah/michelle are you there
in the wings i have lost my history my
voice   and in the dark beneath the stage
i felt the audience burn/my children

standing   we were mute/divided
by the footlights of reality   they
gazed/sweet innocents   i closed my eyes/my
self   i was not right for this part/never
was much of an actress   anyway

compass and map

Gone are all the vines, hands, wells, sills of discontent
the acqua head slipping in its purple pool
Fed up with every network slub you come to like a cross
People are people. I can take them or leave them.
And leave along the white atrocious vales
leaving judicial behind with its tin of promises
the pocked roads leading you from death to furnished death
where friends pull the pont across to them
and unflock every arrow that contains your purpose

Weary and complacent sorrow drives you
to any passing straw. She floats on an exuberant lid of water
Beneath, the roots tug dense and introverted
Blindness drills me in its tub

His favours pull the globe he drenches What a greaser
and where I wrenched he spins
Plato rids me, waiting for the holy boats

that stir across black water
Jazz consoles with minuets
Baffling truth will raise you from his bed
I listen to the scathing drums
the toy wrapped in kid
and blast your travel and your voices on the black bay

bye-bye barbie

A fable of Leah's dolls

Betty with the home-made clothes
glares across the room at Barbie
who is shop-dressed, brand new,
buxom and coolly smiling.

Betty with the home-made hate
sidles across the room on her rag bum
sneakily, bit by bit, so Leah won't see.
She is dragging the toy soldier's axe.

Betty with the built-up hours
of staring across the room
has been inventing stories.
She is calling herself Cinderella

She is calling herself Beauty
and Orphan, and Princess - and right.
Barbie, watching round-eyed, is mesmerised
as Stepmother/Ogre/Troll lunges for her blood.

thirteen

DIANE FAHEY

I was practising being a saint.
My brown lace-ups were clamped
to the dusty floor, and I was in them.
The mirror, an oval drop
of flat untrembling water, showed
a pale girl inside a yellow raincoat.
I hated it. 'This one,' I said.
My mother passed the silky beige one,
the dearer one, back to the woman,
and softly they agreed: 'Too young
to know its value.'
                'Some of us even
wear yellow raincoats to school!'
The nun stood on a bench -
wasp-waisted, her cheeks covered
with tributaries of red lightning.
Her eyes glittered as two hundred girls
marched with military precision
round the playground. In tune
with a deeper instinct, I dragged
my feet into the asphalt,
waiting to be detected, punished....
She was the one who ground me down
the way she ground her yellow teeth,
and almost triumphed -
until the day when, kindled with rage,
she struck me across the arm:
'Get out, then!' And I had won,
my eyes drops of flat untrembling water,
giving her back her hatred,

arachne and the bogeyman

JAN MATTHEWS

THE FLY IN THE WEB at the door is thrashing frantically. Heaving, lurching, threshing feet and wings in a terrible effort. The threads cling, holding him fast. Black and shiny, the spider at the centre waits until the thrashing stops. Then he moves quickly, surefooted on that gossamer death of his. There is a flurry of activity as the fly is stilled and trussed. The master weaver returns to the centre. And waits some more.

I am afraid.

Are you old? I have always been old. Ten years, old. They laugh at me. I am embarrassed. Feel my face go all hot. I want to hide then. Perhaps I am a crazy person. I can't tell. I have nothing to compare. I just know I have always been this old.

Sometimes I want to ask someone, my mother perhaps, what is young. And why aren't I. But sometimes people look at me strangely. Perhaps I am a crazy person. They get put in a place where they can't ever get out. My friends told me that.

I don't like nights. Spiders creep around my bed in the dark. A carpet of them. It moves. My heart thumps and my chest is so tight it is hard to breathe. I clutch my bear. His hair prickles. I shut my eyes tight, so tight the lids will pry my eyeballs loose and then they'll roll around in the black space inside my head.

How can there be shadows in the night? Long tall shadows. They are blacker than the darkness, that is how I know they are there. I can see them. They are always there, now. The shadows and the spiders. The spiders must live in my head. They come out of it when I am asleep and crawl on me, out of my nostrils and my mouth, and my ears. They swarm all over me. One night they will bite me.

So far I have woken up just in time. They are afraid of me when I am awake. They vanish back inside my head. Perhaps if they get me they will go away. Perhaps then they will be satisfied. Sometimes I vanish too. I don't know where I go. But I go somewhere when I'm scared. Perhaps I am dead. But no one else notices. Robbie?

Big hands, man's hands, all of a sudden stroke and grasp, knead my breasts. I can't breathe. Can't move. My heart thumps so hard. Will my head burst? Am I dying? I am afraid. I feel funny down there, nice. But I am so afraid.

I must get away. He is all around me, clinging to my hands, arms, feet, legs. Around my body, my neck. Fight! I must get out! Pull this arm, that leg. Turn over, kick! Kick some more, tear at it! I will get free! The spider! The spider's coming. It's black. It has fangs. Stop. Lie still. I must not move. If I don't move it won't know anyone's caught. Ssh. Quiet. Freeze.

Run the bath. It's a bit cold. Never mind, the water will be warm. Heave for breath, drag it in, gasping. But where's the water? Look! Look at it! Black sharp legs, shiny head. Big fat body. So many legs! When, where can I be safe? Slowly, slowly, get to the plug. Careful, he will get you. No, he's floating to the other end. Quick, pull the plug and swish him down. Go on horrible! Go on, down the drain! Put the plug back in. You won't ever get out.

Check the bed, the walls, the corners, under the bed. Safe, nothing there. Where's my bear. Hold me bear, don't let them get me. You love me, don't you bear?

I have always been old. It's the night that makes me old. I am afraid.

I wonder if my friends are old. I think so. Adults laugh when I say things. Perhaps you're only meant to say some things when you're big. I wonder what mum said in the car today. I heard about the hair growing, and my breasts, and the bleeding. But then I couldn't hear her. Only the car engine, and the wind, the bumps of the tyres. Perhaps I am a crazy person. I couldn't hear her when she said it again either. If I asked her a third time she would really have thought I was stupid. Maybe even crazy. Lucky I realized. You have to be careful. They might send me away to that place where the crazy people are.

I love to swim, feel the strength in my arms, paddling the surfboard. The beach is fun. The sun is all warm, happy light. Everything is tinged, sparkly. Now they won't let me do anything. 'A hyperactive mind,' that's what the doctor said. 'Disturbs her sleep. She's acting out what she does during the day. She can't tell the difference in her sleep. That's why she's thumping the walls and pushing the bed around. Keep her more quiet during the day.' That's all he knows. He's stupid. I'm not doing any more than I ever do. It's not that. Dumb man. But I have to be careful. Perhaps I'm really becoming a crazy person. They'll send me away. Have to do what I'm told. Watch out. Be careful.

I must not move. Still, stay still. It is so dark. Don't move. They'll hear my heart thumping. What? Who's that? Pulling my pyjamas down over my legs. Torch shining on me. Oh please, don't. It hurts. I can't breathe. Your cheeks are so prickly and sharp. Please don't. I can't breathe. Why are you . . . that hurts. Please Robbie . . . .

The spider has moved today. He is in the top corner of his web, spinning his front legs.

Are you making more web, spider?

I can ride, ride for miles and miles. My legs are strong. They push the pedals harder and harder. Faster. I glide, glide in and out, round, down the hills. The sun is just above the buildings, the clouds are pink. It is so lovely. I feel I will burst with it. I soar. Gravel. Watch this! Jam on the brake. Back wheel skids, slews around. Oops, it slides out from under me. Look at my leg. All that blood. I'm strong. I'm brave. Nothing can make me cry. Watch me bash my hand. See the blood? I told you, nothing can make me cry. Nothing. I can hurt myself any way I want, and I can take it. I'm brave. I'm strong. No one can do anything to hurt me that I can't do myself and never even cry a bit.

My friends look at me strangely now. They know things I don't. What is it they know? I can't ask the question because I don't know what it is. Am I stupid? Perhaps. Or crazy. They laugh at me a lot, my friends. Somehow everyone is older than me. They don't understand the safe care of a bear, they don't need the comfort of a light at night. Don't they see shadows in the dark?

I am more used to them now. Sometimes I don't know what's happened, just put my pyjamas back on when I wake up and find them at the bottom of the bed. I gave him a fright one night. Him and his bloody torch. 'What are you doing?' I said to him. He nearly jumped out of his skin. Serves him right. I am strong, tough, now. See, if I cut myself with this Gillette, I don't even flinch. I love scars. They are the signs of strength, marks of bravery. Nothing can hurt me.

But at the door, the fly is bloodsucked, hollow. My spider sits, no fatter, just content. And quiet, now.

a ghost in the kitchen

FRANCES STEPHANS

I WAS FOURTEEN WHEN WAR broke out. Too old to be evacuated. Old enough to leave school. 'You're big enough and ugly enough,' my mother said. 'Grow up!' my brothers told me. I was fifteen when I started work at the telephone exchange. 'War work', they called it. I was 'Doing my bit'.

I'd leave for work very early in the morning, crossing the untidy city. I was old enough to see the mess before it was cleared away - a severed arm dangling from a telegraph wire, a finger defiantly poking through the rubble - waiting to be neatly gathered up and packed away in boxes. So I grew up. It was better that way. I began to wear make-up and bought myself a pair of high-heeled shoes.

The war changed everything for everyone. It became a milestone, something to measure our lives by. Before the war and after the war. Try to forget what happened in between. Before the war I was a child; and children are innocent, aren't they?

My father was in the Navy so we had a fairly comfortable life. That is to say, we were better off than most, though times were hard for everyone.

I can picture my mother in the kitchen. That's where she'd be when we got in from school. Sometimes, after tea, she'd get dressed up and go out. I hated those evenings, alone with my brothers. At their mercy. It would start with teasing, progress to insults, and end up in a brawl. Then I would grab my mac, go down to the station, and sit for hours as the trains rolled in one after another. Finally the last train, and if she was on it I'd get the sharp end of her tongue and a clip across the ear to boot. If she wasn't, I'd walk home alone.

The ghost of my mother is in the kitchen, pacing up and down in the small space between the table and the stove. Pacing; like a hamster in a cage. The ghost of a child, a little girl, sits watching her. On the table is a letter from the girl's father. He only writes when he is coming home. She is feeling sick.

Memories are like ghosts. They come from time to time to haunt me. I wouldn't mind at all if they left me here but they take me with them. Defying time and space they take me back. The sights, sounds and smells of childhood envelop me and I am powerless once more.

Aunt Winnie has come to take me out for the day. 'The sea air will do us good, Darcy.' My brothers are fishing and mother's busy, so we have the whole day all to ourselves. We are sitting on the soft grass near Pearson's Tower, having our picnic. I am staring up at the white spectre of that landlocked lighthouse, surrounded by tarmac and a sea of people, whilst I chew halfheartedly on a marmite sandwich.

I love Auntie Win with all my heart, and I think she likes me. I pretend that she is my mother. Picnic lunches and church on Sunday. I see her tucking me safely into bed at night and stooping down to caress my cheek. 'Oh look, Darcy! A four-leaf clover. Make a wish!' I take an apple from the picnic basket and look back towards the tower. Its whiteness is dazzling and I have to shield my eyes with my hand.

A woman jumped to her death from that tower. She must have done it in broad daylight as you have to pay tuppence to get to the top. They say she was going to have a baby. There's something awfully bad about babies. I'm trying not to think of her as we sit there eating but it's no use. My ears fill with the shocked screams of the onlookers: I hear the sickening crunch. The pure white tower is spattered with crimson and blood is pouring from her open skull onto the tarmac. Auntie Win offers me hot sweet tea from a vacuum flask. I drink it and immediately feel sick. I remember that my father is coming home.

Dark shadows appear on the grass and sweep towards us. The sky is crowding over. We get up and shake the crumbs from our skirts. 'Would you like to climb to the top of the tower, Darcy? No? We'll go for a walk then, shall we?' As we pass the tower I glance down at the tarmac and wonder who scrubbed off the stains.

We walk along the waterfront as storm-clouds gather and the sea turns grey. I badly need to spend a penny but I won't tell Aunt Winifred; you can catch things off lavatory seats. It's cold now, and I'm feeling miserable. Auntie Win doesn't look happy either. She stops and leans against the railings, staring blankly out to sea. She is somewhere far away from me. Somewhere in the grown-up world. I look at the horizon and think of my father out there. 'Worse things happen at sea, Darcy.' I know. I don't doubt it.

Memories are like fools - we must suffer them gladly. I want to turn and run but if I do the ghosts will pursue me.

I am standing in the kitchen doorway watching a strange woman in the backyard. She is tending a bonfire, poking at a bundle of rags she has thrown into the centre of the fire. They are bloodstained. 'Ask no questions and you'll be told no lies.' The acrid smoke is stinging my eyes. 'She's had an accident, your mother has. Fell downstairs and hurt her back. Don't you go bothering her now. She'll be right as rain in a day or two.'

After tea I'm sent to bed. I pause outside my mother's room, wondering if I should go in and say goodnight. The door is slightly ajar and I hear the soft murmur of Auntie Win's voice making comforting noises. Then my mother's voice, devoid of emotion. 'It was a boy.' I stand there feeling like a criminal, wanting to hear more but nothing more is said.

I am lying on my bed in the darkness, trying to piece the day together like a jigsaw - there are pieces missing. Who was the boy? What had he done? I had wished upon a clover but I hadn't meant to hurt her. I creep under my bed and lie there on the cold hard floor, feeling like a murderer. I know I am bad. I can't help it.

A ghost is in the kitchen. It is the ghost of my father, home from the sea. The ghost of a child, a little girl, stands staring at him. On the table is a box of sweets, a present from her father. 'Come and give your Da a kiss then, Darcy.' Her stomach tightens. She is feeling sick.

RAE LUCKIE

in the city

NELL LIVED IN SYDNEY. Alone.
She wrote great letters.
(Tons and tons of love, Nell.)

And sent me books and *Women's Weekly*, *Woman's Own* and *New Idea*. Bundled in brown paper. Tied with string. Addressed in blue copperplate.

Miss Patsy Rae Kelly
c/- Mrs W H Marston
72 Clinton Street
Orange

In the early days I lived with her during school holidays. If you want to see where she lived, catch a tram from Central to St James. Stand in the vestibule. Face Elizabeth Street.
    Just before the train enters the tunnel under Goulburn Street, look up, you can see the sign. 'Low Priced Accommodation'. Aranui Lodge, but it used to be called Wentworth House. If you look really hard you can still see the faint painted white letters on the corner brickwork. Wentworth House Residential.

Her room
last one
second floor
around the corner
above Wentworth lane

There used to be a box with geraniums. Only on her window sill.
    Single room 12 x 8 second floor single bed eighteen years of living bath down the hall dingy shabby creaking caged lift smell of cooking people who go and ask for towels. Not the permanents. Bath must be scrubbed out with Rinso before use. Don't talk to anyone. Here's your key. Don't lose it. Bare element in metal dish sausages tomato and onions single bed. Black coffee cigarettes and Vincents APC. Centre of the room bare light bulb dangling on twisted cord.
    Watching the trains the parking station being built noise of jack-hammers cranes traffic sirens. Another suicide in Wentworth Lane they jump from Mansion House. Don't look.
    Meet me after work read dawdle down to Hyde Park for a while. Past Mark Foys. Elegant slim women immobilised in glass cages. Stand on DJ's corner. Listen to the trams, the cars, the buses, the sirens. Look for her as each load of people spew from St James station entrance and fan to the right and left, across the street or up the broad walk towards the fountain in Hyde Park. She's not there. Go into DJ's. Ride the rattling wooden escalators up. Anticipate the jump off. What if I get caught and sucked down underneath.
    (Children under twelve must be accompanied by an adult but I'm big so big for my age.)
    Ride the lift down. Ground floor says the man in uniform.
    Back to wait on the corner. Bustling feet. Police on horses herding pedestrians. Fresh smell of sweet manure. (Mind where you walk.) There she is. A cigarette-in-hand wave as she awaits the white helmet's signal. 'Come on hurry up. Quit gawping up at the buildings, you look like a country bumpkin.' I like the one that looks like my tin money box. Bank Commonwealth.

She worked at Central Railway. The only woman, one of the men. Women clean and caretake the toilets and collect tickets but Nell was the first woman to sell them. Had to make a new category 'Special Class Female Clerk'. Didn't get paid the same as a man of course. But a woman in a man's job. All her life.

Every holidays dragged me around Central to meet people. Waiting until the barrier quietened. Up and down each set of stairs. Stairs with specks of blackish silver sparkling in the grey cement. Tweak my blond plaits. Gidday love. Hasn't she grown! Dancing lessons eh? Learning the piano eh? Nice to see yer again dear. Are you going to the beach? Doesn't she look like you. She's a big girl they say. Nell hates big girls.

Central underground. Bronze barred window. On either side racks of coloured tickets for every destination waiting to be plunged with an in and out clank into the dating machine ready primed with purple ink. Cachoong Cachoong. Once each end for a return. Broken fingernails mended with sticking plaster, drawers full of pounds shillings and pence waiting to be counted. Queues of impatient customers. Time for a break. Cigarette black coffee and a Vincents APC. Carefully unfold the wrapper and straighten. Bend it crossways. Tip the pink tangy powder into a pile on the end of your tongue. Drink and swallow with a thrust up of the chin. Back to the neverending queue of impatient customers.

For eighteen years.

The gun for protection on split night shifts. 'I'd never use it,' she said, 'they can take the money for all I care.' How is she game to walk home alone in the dark of the night in the middle of the city? (Smell the brewery.) I'd be so scared but I'm not when I'm with her. I keep close but she doesn't hold my hand. Skipping steps trying to keep up with her city walk. I prefer to dawdle. But she grips my arm when we dash across the street. Back to the poky room with the bathroom down the hall. We top and tail in the single bed. She wears Shranks cotton pyjamas.

She lived there eighteen years.

I listen to the noises and smell the smells.

Only one building frightened me. The dental hospital near Central

Railway. Just up from Wentworth House where she lived. The dental hospital. You couldn't avoid going past it. Every day. Legs tremble, heart beats, stomach hurts. Panic. First teeth rotten. They don't count. Second teeth. Getting rotten. 'You must go to the dentist,' Nell said. 'There's nothing to be scared of.' But I didn't and I was.

Once I get home she'll foget about it. I promise I'll go to the dentist when I get back to Orange. Don't make me go the the dental hospital. Please Please Please Nell I'll go as soon as I get home. 'Well if you don't next holidays I'm taking you to the dental hospital.' There's a room full of dentists' chairs and they sit you in all together and the people learning to be dentists practise on you and they hurt and you can see everyone else getting hurt. 'They'll yank all yer teeth out. With big pliers.'

I promise I'll go when I get home I promise I promise.

The spidery neon sign blinks Cahills Restaurant. Quartered glass ushers customers in waiting to be seated. 'Come on,' says Nell. I step in quickly behind her. In the same section of the revolving door. Our feet touch. Nell tries to save herself but we land in a tangled heap at the feet of the laughing waitress.

Nell is silent. I look at my crunchy honey coloured toasted waffle. Thick rivulets of rich brown caramel sauce coursing down creamy white ice-cream. The circular waffle is scored in four places. Just like the door I think. I cut the ice-cream in four and carefully spread it to fill in the squares in the waffle. Then I cut it piece by piece with the knife and fork and swirl it in the sauce until the crispness goes dripping and soggy. It trickles down the front of the yellow bolero Nell knitted me. Decorated each side with pink hair clip bows covered in blue raised dots. You could take them out to wash it. The bolero smelt like Nell. 'Will you stop playing with that waffle and eat it!' she snaps as she drinks black coffee and has a cigarette and a Vincents APC.

'Don't you ever be so stupid again!' she yells when we are alone.

Next time we went to Repins.

Down to the Strand Arcade for some Vienna almonds to take home to Madge. Coffee in Miss Nancy's crowded shop. Back up to Central. Smell the brewery. Smell the underground. To the Tiv up in the gods. Magic. Better than the pictures. Each trip a treat she always had tickets for a live show.

Her body was found after nine days. I open the door. No-one warns the mess a body leaves. Continuous ming blue curtaining caressing the geraniums. Chimes tinkling. (To keep away the bad spirits.) Shelf with two gold cartons of Benson and Hedges and one of Vincents APC. Green skirt and jacket and navy blouse slung over a chair. Navy court Sandlers and matching shoulder bag on the floor. Coffee table. Two chop bones on a plate. Writing pad. Half scrawled letter. Game of patience on the floor. She used to sit knees bent with arms curled around. Jelly and custard in the fridge.

I have to get away from the smell. Nilodor Glen 20 Pine O Kleen White King Bleach.

Everyone busy and bustling in Elizabeth Street. Hear the trains smell the brewery. I want to stand and scream and tell them that Nell is dead. I want to stop the world. Just for a minute. She was lying dead when I tried to ring and I didn't know.

On or about 2/11/77
Intra cerebral haemorrhage
Hypertension
Inquest dispensed with at Glebe
Cremated 15/11/77
F D Crowe, Coroner's Delegate.

She never said she loved me.

But she wrote great letters.

Tons and tons of love, Nell.

in the early afternoon

SOMETIMES WHEN I HAVE PUT the baby down for the afternoon, I leave the house. I slip out through a loose paling in the back fence. There is just room enough for me, and when I am through and out into the empty block on the other side I put the paling back in place.

The grass is long there, and I feel it on my legs, even through the thick cotton material of my pants. I think about the block being sold finally. The grass will be cut. I imagine the men on their lawnmowers and the sad sound of the wind over the naked ground.

It is early afternoon when I go. I am gone for ten, fifteen minutes, no more than half an hour.

It is the quiet of the afternoon. There is washing on the line, on all the neighbourhood lines that back onto the empty block. There are old ladies' underpants, toddlers' jumpsuits, nappies on other lines. I think of my daughter but I do not glance back. As I cross the empty block I think of the loose paling behind me, waiting for me, allowing me this time away.

I think it is a time of discovery, this being away, this being on my own. I know I will carry stories back to my daughter in the house. But to find them I walk the neighbourhood alone.

The stillness haunts me. Later at night when there is a different stillness around me, I remember the soothing sun-filled quiet of early afternoon. It is a comfortable suburban sound. I imagine I will remember it for years to come when other forces, other constraints, will not allow me to experience it first-hand, in solitude. I imagine speaking of it when my daughter is 'grown'. Will she forgive me when I talk of what I have done? Will she understand my stepping away from her in search of stories, things to share, time alone? Will she go out to the back fence then and hunt for the loose paling?

I kick stones along the footpath as I walk - tiny skipping stones that bounce off into the grass, where I bend down to search for them and slip them into the pocket of my cardigan. I am seen, sometimes, looking in the grass, and I blush at the inquisitive 'Lost something?' Do they know me, these people? Will they tell?

I will add the stones to the collection. I will empty my pockets when I go back to the house. Stones, twigs, bits of silver foil, wrappings from lollies, a paddlepop stick engraved with the letter *L*. I keep them in an old chocolate tin in the back of a drawer in my daughter's room.

Other things I cannot carry in my pocket. The neighbourhood is so new to me, though we have lived here for some years. I seem to be seeing it for the first time, in these last few months. I turn corners and I am lost. The houses, the lawns, the inhabitants of my neighbourhood - I have not known them before. I am a stranger. I watch, enthralled.

I come upon a park. It is a small reserve no more than a few streets from the house. But I stumble upon it as if I have stepped in from another world. I have not known of its existence. *Dorothy Reserve*, the sign says. I think: It is my mother's park, named for my mother. There is a children's swing, a slippery dip, a merry-go-round. A path, worn through the grass, winds down from a gap in the low wooden fence. I am too early for the children who will come later in the afternoon. But in the park, in my mother's reserve, I rest for a while - just a minute or two - on a bench. The sun is on my face and I let it stay. I let it reach into me. There is a breeze that lifts the hair at my neck. And in the comfort of both forces, the warmth and the cool air, I feel refreshed, rested. It is time then to go home.

The wind turns a little as I head home. Women in their front gardens cling suddenly to their sun-hats. I see their garden-gloved hands, their indistinct, shadowed smiles. I think that there are always the others looking in.

I am a good mother, I know. I am told. I tell myself again as I walk back across the empty block. 'You are doing well,' they tell me, even my mother who I cannot hope to emulate.

'How did you do it?' I ask her again and again 'With so many?' She is gentle, unassuming in her reply. She does not say how, does not seem to know. 'I just did,' she says, 'I just did'.

I do not know her - this young woman in the photos, laughing, dark-haired - summer backyard shots - in a sleeveless dress, my father in a singlet, toddlers, babies in nappies. My mother's arms are white, smooth. Her breasts are full. The sun is on her shoulders. The southerly wind, heading for the back fence behind her, lifts the hair from her face. I search for her tiredness but in my wonder at her looks, her youth, her strangeness, I cannot see anything else. Until, walking back across the empty block, damp underfoot, the long grass catching in the cuffs of my pants, I remember.

My sisters and I were surprised, disbelieving when she mentioned, as if in passing, how she had left us sometimes. 'When you were asleep ...' she said. 'Not for long... just up to the shop....' I have the memory of her words failing, fading as she spoke. There was the hesitation, I remember, the just-dawning realization that she needed to defend. And I had made her feel that need, that burden of explanation. I, reacting in anger, before my daughter was born, cried 'How could you?' And my mother, as if she had given something of herself away and regretted it now, became quiet. 'I just did.'

I think of how it must have seemed to her that I was testing, questioning her love, this woman I did not, do not know, though I am growing closer every day.

The afternoon sun is warm on my face again. The *For Sale* sign on the edge of the block is tilting to one side. It is giving way in the damp earth so that soon the long grass will obscure the words. But I do not wait to see. I think of the house, ahead of me now, inviting. The land slopes down towards it. I see two women talking in the yard of the house next door. They are like two figures on a screen, turning as the camera moves in. I know they are watching me, wondering.

And I know too that it is love for my daughter that calls me back through the long grass, as much as it is love that calls me, in the early afternoon, towards the loose paling in the back fence. It is not a question of my being a good mother.

Yet I cannot avoid the thought of the calls while I have been away. Someone will have called.

There will be calls later. Concerned, worried, afraid. Their voices saying 'I called . . . it rang and rang . . . . Where were you?' But I will tell them 'Out in the yard', 'In the laundry', 'With the baby . . . .'

I lie, not so much to conceal, but to avoid the explanation. I will keep it from them all, even from my husband, who would, I know, try to understand. But it is mine, and I guard it carefully.

Only my daughter will know.

When I return to the house, I go to her. After my walk around the neighbourhood there is a gentleness in my step. I feel it myself. I am no longer quite so weary. Her breathing is steady, clear. She is sleeping; she has not missed me while I have been gone. She stirs when I touch the warm pink of her cheek. In sleep, she reaches to hold my finger, listens as I talk to her. 'Go on,' she is telling me. I reach into the pocket of my cardigan. I show her what I have found to add to our collection - stick, marble, stone, a piece of blue fallen from the sky.

'A park,' I tell her. 'Today I found a park . . . *Dorothy Reserve* . . . after your grandmother . . . to think, all this time, it's only been a few streets away . . . . Fancy that, just fancy . . .' and she hears her grandmother's expression of wonder and I know she is laughing in her sleep.

The phone rings. As I move to answer it I am already preparing the lie . . . 'Out in the yard . . . .' And I am keeping the other still, quiet inside me.

pretty deadly tidda business

I REMEMBER ALL MY MOTHER'S STORIES, probably much better than she realises. Not only have I heard them a hundred times over but she is a fine story-teller, recalling every event of her life with the vividness of the present, noting each detail right down to the cut and colour of her dress.

I remember her stories of being only allowed to go to Fourth Grade at school; stories of the cohesiveness of Murries on the reserve; stories of how none of them ever saw the money which was paid into their trust accounts. The stories continued when she met and married my father, who was incarcerated as a POW on the Burma-Thailand Railway in the days long before he and his people were even citizens of this country; stories of the excitement of the 1967 Referendum and how Aboriginal[1] people were politically organising themselves; stories of the love and loss of her family. Yes, I too have lived through every one of those feelings as she relates them to me.

---

[1] The term 'Aboriginals' will be used as a noun (as well as adjectively) as it is my preference and political stance as opposed to the word 'Aborigines' which has been used as a term to classify and demean Aboriginal people in the repressive State in which I live, Queensland. 'Aborigines' also assumes an air of superiority by a dominant culture. The terms 'half-caste' and 'full-blood' are biologically racist definitions which are unacceptable to most Aboriginal people today. They have been used as a divide-and-rule tactic by the colonisers.

Recording the memories of elderly Aboriginals is an urgent task, otherwise much information about australian history will be lost forever. The life stories of older people illuminate much about what it was like to live in earlier days, how people experienced the world they knew, and the strategies they developed for coping which have led to present survival. They create a picture of what it has been to be 'on the other side' of forced assimilationist policies.

Aboriginal writing is deeply concerned with precise knowledge of the history of Aboriginal existence, gleaned if necessary from white records, and prised out of white archives. Although archives and documents are white inventions, Aboriginal writers have developed a stronger sense of history than their white counterparts, along with a more intense concern for social reality - with the existence lived by Aboriginal people today and in the past.

In attempting to provide an analysis of writing my Mother's life, it is necessary to elucidate the vital role oral history plays in the recording of Aboriginal stories and how it has changed over the years, specifically in Queensland where she and her family lived.

In the 1920s the Queensland government pushed tribes out of their traditional areas and placed them onto mission stations and government reserves, ostensibly to protect them from whites but in reality to place them under the control of missionaries and government officials. Traditional customs and practices such as corroborees, ceremonies, religious beliefs and marriage laws, as well as the use of tribal languages, were condemned and actively discouraged by missionaries and managers.

Ever since those forced movements, firstly from traditional areas in the 1920s and then from isolated communities in the 1940s and 1950s, Aboriginal people have become increasingly dispersed into rural towns and cities, resulting in the continued fragmentation of Aboriginal history and oral tradition. When people were living together in larger and enclosed communities history and tradition were passed on orally by the older ones, and while the community remained together traditions were maintained. This was one of the many resistance strategies that Aboriginals employed against the colonising forces.

The Queensland government's long-term plan was to eventually absorb Aboriginal people into the white community so that Aboriginal people and their cultures would become extinct. This plan did not succeed, and it is a testament to the power of the Aboriginal sense of history that Aboriginal people have been able to withstand these deliberate forces of complete annihilation. Aboriginal people still have a rich tradition of oral history, story-telling, philosophy, autobiography and biography, stored particularly by the older people.

Aboriginal studies are now concerned with the transformation of that 'oral literature' into a written literature, without necessarily destroying the original form in the process. Through writing, material that was previously contained to a large extent in a particular local or regional setting becomes available for more general distribution and reinterpretation.

Research by Aboriginal people tends to be concerned with discovering particular matters relating to individuals or communities; requires that the observer be an insider; and recognises that observations depend on the relationship between the observer and observed and also on the particular time and circumstances of the observation. These concerns have shaped my writing of Rita's story.

Rita Huggins was born Rita Holt on August 10th, 1921 at Carnarvon Gorge via Springsure, Central Queensland. She was born of two 'half-caste' parents, Albert and Rose Holt, whose traditional Bidgara-Pitjara area encompassed what is now known as the national park of Carnarvon Gorge.

Rita was never given a tribal name that she could recall. She may have been given one, but it would most certainly have become redundant when her family was forcibly removed to Barambah (as Cherbourg was known in the late 1920s). This redundancy was due to the white expectation that Aboriginal people would no longer continue their 'heathen' ways and practices, and concomitant attempts to Anglicise every aspect of their culture and lifestyle. The prime signifier of personal identification was concealed. As were Albert and Rose, so too were Rita's brothers and sisters prescribed European names - Barney, Margaret, Clare, Harry, Thelma, Rita, Jimmy, Lawrence, Violet, Ruby, Oliver, Albert, Isobel and Walter.

Anguish and confusion surrounded the Holt family as they awoke one morning to the clamour of horses and troopers riding through their camp. Rita remembers her mother shielding the children protectively from the troopers as her father cautiously investigated. Soon after they were transported in the back of a cattle truck to Barambah.

Vividly she recalls her grandmother wailing as the 'mob' were rounded up. 'Don't take my gunduburris![2] Don't take my gunduburris!' she screamed repeatedly. Much later Rita was told that her aged grandmother wandered off aimlessly into the bush that day, and was never sighted alive again. It is presumed she died alone somewhere out there with a broken heart. When her body was found it was taken to Woorabinda where her 'full-blood' relations lived.

On the basis of skin colour the 'half-castes' were sent to Barambah and the 'full-bloods' sent to Woorabinda, in accord with the colonisers' ideology that children who possessed strains of white blood would be easier to assimilate than their darker counterparts. The lighter-skinned children were also segregated from the darker children in classes to accelerate their acceptance as white people. Teachers and missionaries were astounded when this strategy did not succeed.

Schooling was the primary location for Aboriginal children to be socialised and imbued with European education. Rita attended school from the age of eight to the age of thirteen, or fourth grade as it was then. Subjects taken were basic reading, writing and arithmetic, with particular emphasis on British History, Captain Cook and sewing. Happy memories of school still remain with Rita, not because of the educational content, but because it was a place where kids could socialise.

Outside of school other duties took precedence. As one of the middle ones in the family, Rita undertook most of the jobs her brothers and sisters performed. The egalitarian nature of family relationships was such that no-one had specific jobs or ever felt 'picked on'. At a very young age Rita helped gather firewood as well as attending to other chores which included washing up, cleaning the yard, helping prepare dinner and looking after younger brothers and sisters while her mother rested.

Rita was sent to the mission dormitory at the relatively late age of thirteen as punishment for dating boys. The life in the dormitories was one of control, regimentation and discipline, where boys and girls were segregated and all were required to do a range of domestic chores such as making their beds, rinsing soiled linen, washing and scrubbing out the dormitory and picking up papers. After breakfast the children would go to school for several hours. Some play time filled in the rest of the day before prayers, dinner and bed.

2. Aboriginal word for children

The dormitories segregated children from their parents as a strategy of social control, which did its damage in its attempts to sever ties between the children and their traditional life. The considerable time absorbed by dormitory routine succeeded in limiting the depth and richness of the children's traditional knowledge. Dormitory life also attempted to take away the disciplinary powers of the children's natural parents. Aboriginals now were being managed, protected, taught and chastised like children and in this way lost much of the autonomy they formerly enjoyed.

Rita never felt that Cherbourg was her home, and she yearned nostalgically for the days she had known in Carnarvon Gorge. A dislocated person in a sense, she was physically located at Barambah but emotionally and spiritually located in Carnarvon Gorge. Unlike an immigrant to a new country, Rita would not and could not entertain the notion that she had chosen to relinquish her place of birth for 'greener pastures'. Her soul stirred for her traditional lands. She felt an outcast, a refugee in her own country, like so many other Aboriginals in the past, present and future.

Around the age of thirteen or fourteen the time came for girls to serve apprenticeships to train as 'worthy housekeepers' and Rita remembers the expectation of all the girls, whether they were of her age group or younger, that they would fulfil the role of domestic servants. It was routine for girls to be placed in servitude as domestic servants by certain persons in authority. The Aboriginals' Preservation and Protection Acts 1939-1946 empowered reserve superintendents to enter employment contracts on behalf of residents, to hold any funds residents might have and to control residents' spending. The then Cherbourg superintendent had arrangements with both local and distant policemen, pastoralists and farmers to supply a steady flow of workers for those in 'need'.

Rita's first job in 1934 entailed a long day from dawn until the late hours of the evening in the daily routine of cleaning, washing, ironing, preparing food and caring for the children. She performed domestic work for many years, before and after the birth of her children. Her background and her experience of work as a domestic has, in a way, shaped her lifestyle: even today she does not feel comfortable and a 'whole' person unless she has spent the day in some kind of domestic activity, whether it be cooking or cleaning.

In 1940, when she was eighteen years old, Rita met Jack Huggins in

Brisbane. In the 1940s he was possibly the first Aboriginal person in Queensland to hold a position in the Post Office. It was not until after World War II that Rita and Jack re-met, marrying in 1951 in Ayr, North Queensland. Their union produced three children - two girls and a boy. Rita already had two girls from a previous relationship. However, never fully recovering from his war injuries, Jack's life with his young family was brief. He died in 1958 from a heart attack at the age of thirty-eight.

Devastated by the loss of her husband, Rita returned to Brisbane in 1959 to the comfort of her extended family network. Her family was one of the first Aboriginal families to live in Inala, now the most densely populated Aboriginal suburb in Brisbane. As the population expanded, many Aboriginal people formed their own identifiable community groups. Rita excelled at providing a way for local Aboriginal families who were new to the city to get to know each other. She was able to operate in this manner largely under the umbrella of OPAL.

OPAL, the One People of Australia League, was formed in 1961 in response to changed political circumstances. During the era of Labor rule in Queensland (1915-1957) no independent Aboriginal voices were ever officially allowed to surface and make themselves heard. Not a single statement from an Aboriginal was ever reproduced in Parliament, in printed government reports or in the media. Not until the change of government in 1957 did the opportunity arise to form an organisation of Aboriginals and non-Aboriginals with the support of government.

Legislation within Queensland had been predominantly paternalistic and with the new interest in minorities, coming mainly from the American civil rights movement, the Queensland government found itself on the defensive because of the upsurge of interest in Aboriginal rights. A possible reason for the evolution of OPAL was that the Country/Liberal Party Government found it useful to generate an organisation which could be used as a showcase of public support for Government policies, an organisation made up of welfare-oriented, rather than politically-oriented people. OPAL enjoyed close relations with the Queensland government and received some government funds. Indeed two members of the OPAL Board were senior public servants in the Department of Native Affairs.

Not all organisations concerned with Aboriginal affairs had the support of the government. The Queensland Council for the Advancement of Aborigines and Torres Strait Islanders (QCAATSI), formed in

1960, fought continuously for civil rights and was critical of the Queensland government. Along with other left-wing Aboriginal groups in Queensland, QCAATSI claimed that OPAL was a government front comprised of tame cats.

It was the third of OPAL's stated objectives - 'to weld the coloured and white citizens of Australia into *One People*' - reeking of the assimilationist philosophies of the day, which led to OPAL immediately being viewed as a pro-government, pro-assimilationist organisation. In spite of these criticisms, many Aboriginal people gained social and political confidence from OPAL. An opportunity to work for Aboriginal welfare, outside the political arena but encouraged by the government, was an attractive proposition for the early members of OPAL.

Rita was known as the 'glamour girl' of OPAL. She was an Aboriginal woman who presented herself in a dignified and commanding manner, full of confidence and self-assurance, who defied and was the ultimate exception to Aboriginal stereotypes existing at the time. She knew firmly who she was and what she was and where she stood as an Aboriginal person and a facilitator between two cultures which were like chalk and cheese: the oppressed and oppressor. This is a difficult line to tread, but Rita did so with ease and grace.

Within OPAL a cooperative and comfortable working relationship existed with whites. Rita recalls the hours spent listening to white people speaking. She was impressed by how they conducted themselves and she learnt a great deal from these interactions. This is what essentially appealed to Rita, a great humanitarian who 'loves' all people of every colour, race and creed. She talked excitedly about her family, people and culture to those who had never encountered an Aboriginal before. First impressions may be the greatest, and Rita has never relinquished her starring role as the Aboriginal people's Ambassadress.

Aboriginals in Brisbane were faced not only with the usual difficulties of newcomers but also with those of rural or small town people moving into an urban area. Additionally, Aboriginals were faced with problems engendered by racial prejudice and discrimination. Attesting to this, Rita and her family moved house fourteen times in three years, largely because of discrimination by landlords in renting premises to Aboriginals and their intolerance of the sharing of homes with transient or homeless relatives and friends.

This did not deter Rita from helping others. Rita would voluntarily assist newly-arrived Aboriginal people from reserves and country areas in contacting the Housing Commission, applying for benefits from Social Security, being placed in contact with relations, gaining access to schools for their children, applying for employment - an overall information and access billboard.

Inala is a low socio-economic Brisbane suburb and was particularly so in the early 1960s and it is interesting to note that the 'poor whites' in the neighbourhood also gravitated to Rita's house. She was able to assist them, always insisting that OPAL 'helps both blacks and whites in need'. Food parcels, Christmas presents and holiday camps were some of the offerings extended to many families in the Inala region. Rita thus became OPAL's official agent in the area. A former friend would joke that Rita would 'go opalling' occasionally, meaning that she would spread the good word of OPAL as far as possible, acting as a talent scout, recruiting some, and 'educating' people about the aims and objectives of OPAL.

As Rita's children, OPAL was a large and sometimes annoying part of our lives, being constantly dragged around to dances, socials and talks on Aboriginal culture. Always displaying her very deep sense of pride in her Aboriginality, Rita was able to instil this in her children by talking for hours to other people about Aboriginals in the halls of OPAL. She not only educated others but also her own children to respect Aboriginal people and to recognise that they had worthy contributions to make to society.

OPAL instilled a positive feeling that has made an enormous impact on Rita and her family's life. Meeting Aboriginals and empathetic non-Aboriginals has provided lasting friendships, not only for Rita's generation but for her children's. Not only did the OPAL experience equip Rita and her children with social skills, but it provided us all with a political framework from which to operate.

Yes, I too have lived through every one of those feelings as she related them to me. By virtue of being Rita's daughter, and a close one at that, I possess many of her experiences.

However as Rita is a product of her time, so too am I. Some of the things she may have been obliged to accept in those days (I say obliged here, as I feel she has never accepted anything), particularly the blatant patronisation, discrimination and subjugation, are like waving a red flag at a bull to me. Not that she never had the courage to stand up for herself; the plain fact was, every obstacle was placed in her way and if she objected she would have faced the barrage of insults and humiliation thrown at Aboriginal people in those days. I'm not saying that this doesn't occur today but the players, rules and games are different, although there isn't a level playing field yet. Aboriginal people can more easily manipulate the system now. In those days you had to shut up and put up for survival's sake.

So how do 'the oppressed' write about 'the oppressed'? I tried asking this question at a recent conference on autobiography and biography with little success. I guess it's one I have to figure out for myself, but to start with, I would consider it 'the liberated' writing about 'the liberated'.

As for my Mother's wishes, she wants to make the book as accessible to family and Aboriginal community members as possible. And in her words 'This means no big words, little [conscious] politics and my story.' Now this is where my ego takes a bruising because yes, it is her story, not mine. I have to constantly remind myself of that fact.

How much is 'I' the writer? It's a bit like schizophrenia, I guess. Or is it being just plain childish - always wanting to do the opposite when told something? Then I think maybe someone else should have written Rita's life story, but neither she nor I could ever have conceded that one. I believe she has had enough tampering in her life by whites and needs no further investigation or intrusion.

Rita Huggins' biography will be typical of the new phenomenon of contemporary Aboriginal writing where a task lies ahead, not only in addressing personal histories and life stories, but in achieving a more equitable representation for Aboriginal women's history. The title of her book will be *Auntie Rita*, the term she is affectionately known by. It is a sign not only of extended family and community relations but given in the greatest respect to elders of our social world.

My search has been for what I can give my Mother in return for her love, strength, wisdom and inspiration to me. I have found the answer in writing her biography. Her contribution to australia has been immense. She may not have been a public figure the way someone like Charles Perkins has, but she has been a public figure to family and Aboriginal community groups, and to her this is where it counts. She has certainly been the inspiration of my life.

Her life history *is* important, indeed *precious*, and the act of recording and publishing it is, in Aboriginal English, 'pretty deadly tidda business' - which translated means wonderful, strong Black woman stuff.

for the record

SARA HARDY

[A comfortable living room in a small house near Aireys Inlet. Photographs on the wall trace the decades of a woman's theatrical career. There are two fat elderly dogs by the fire. A young woman sits with a cassette tape recorder which she directs towards Frankie, a rounded, grey haired woman of about seventy. Frankie speaks.]

On my own? No. Not always. Well, not really. There was one woman. Well, there've been a few, you know, somehow or other! But only Lydia really, she was the one. We didn't have long, but.... Happy? My word, happy. I'd give my whole life for those few years ....

You ever heard of ENSA? No, you're too young. We entertained the troops during the second war. Different units used to tour - well all over the world really. A lot of Australians were caught in England at the outbreak of the war, and we both happened to join ENSA. That's how we met. She tickled the ivories and I tickled their fancies. Poor bastards. We kept finding ourselves billeted in the same bedroom. Funny that.... Then it was the same bed. They gave us a double bed! Well in them days you took what was given, and anyway it was perfectly innocent. *We* were perfectly innocent.

I tell you - that first time, thrust into bed with the woman I loved. I didn't know where to put myself! Course I knew there was *something* going on between us. I mean you know, don't you - something ... zingy, going on. But then, maybe I didn't know. Because you see we had no role models, no examples, you didn't see it in the streets like you do now. All you had was *The Well of Loneliness* to go on. I cried at the end of that book, I cried and cried. Poor Stephen I thought, that's me, that is *me*. But I cried with relief too, to find that book - even if I did have to cover it with a brown paper wrapper! You did you know, that book was still banned when I read it. It's out of fashion now but it saved a lot of lives that book. At least you knew you were something, not the-only-one-in-the-world. Because you did, you thought that. Each one in her well of loneliness.

Anyway, so there I was in bed with Lydia, middle of the war you know, 'do or die' mentality, and I thought - do something Frankie, *do* something! But I didn't have a clue did I! I mean, it doesn't say what you do in the book does it. They kiss I think - yes, on the mouth, I'm pretty sure there was one of those.... Have you read it? Oh you should. I'll lend it you - bit of lesbian history that after all. *[Frankie looks for the book]*

Eh? Oh Lydia, yes, well... I was certain there was something, you know, between us. But you can't be sure can you, I mean your imagination lets rip and you fantasise so much you think suddenly - this is crazy, I've made it all up, this woman simply likes me!

Friendship, it's a wonderful thing. However much you're in love you don't want to ruin that do you. These days it's different, people don't get quite so shocked. If you play your cards right you can hang onto the friendship - and if you can't, well it wasn't worth having in the first place. But those days, make the wrong move with a woman and you'd be an outcast, you'd want to beg for the firing squad! You were so oppressed, locked in, silent.

I suppose all that was going through my mind as I lay there... that and trying not to sweat! She was very funny. She kept making all these silly jokes and I tried to laugh but my face was so tight I thought I had lock-jaw. She was lovely, lovely, chatting away there, laughing, giggling, bouncing up and down in the bed - all 'girls together having fun' sort of thing. And I was thinking, if I stretch my arm out, you know, casually across her pillow. Pardon? Naked? Naked! Neck to toe nighties dear, neck to toe nighties, buttons at the cuffs. No, you got dressed to go to bed in my day - especially if it was with someone else!

Anyway, Lydia's sitting up doing her impersonation of Ethel Smythe conducting an orchestra with a toothbrush, and I think 'now or never', so I casually slide my arm out across her pillow and sort of lie there you know, looking a right fool! Anyway, Lydia conducts the grande finale, and she's in quite a lather because she impersonates all the instruments as well, see, and suddenly she throws her toothbrush in the air and gracefully falls back, perfectly, into my one arm embrace. And before I could say the immortal words 'fancy a cuddle', she was on me! Rolled right on top of me and kissed me on the mouth. She was kissing me, and I was kissing her, and it was everything, all at once, hands, mouths, arms, legs, lips, everywhere, all over, urgent, passionate - a rummaging mass of whirl. It was wonderful! We didn't know what we were doing but by Hecate we did it! Bed full of buttons in the morning.

We had two wonderful years. Middle of war time but - talk about happy. I don't know what happened. Misunderstandings, jealousies, pressure . . . just call me Stephen! One day I found myself watching her get married. From the back, you know, she didn't see me. Don't know why I went . . . . We didn't keep in touch after that. Too painful.

Yes, it was sad . . . . I would hear about her now and then, you know, 'round the traps. She had kiddies. Still played piano a bit. I spotted her in the audience once - talk about drying! You don't know that word? Forgetting your lines on stage - corpsing is when you laugh. She didn't come backstage afterwards. I waited, but no show.

Do you want a cup of tea? Something stronger? I'm going to. I don't like drinking on me own. *[Gets bottle and glasses]* Well anyway, you know those wobble filters in the films, when time passes - well Time Passes and it's seven years ago and there's a knock on that door and there's Lydia. Forty years on but it's Lydia I'm looking at, just the same, nearly the same. 'I've got a bottle in my bag' she says 'can I come in?' Well she was in! Talk! Talk. We just fell right in, you know, as if time had been nothing. She showed me photos. We told our stories. She already knew half of mine. She'd followed my career, kept a scrapbook and everything. She knew more about me than I did! She'd enjoyed her family . . . she hadn't been bitter, or unhappy, just . . . well, sort of profoundly sad, over what might have been, you know? If we'd understood ourselves better . . . had the courage.

Well she sat in that chair there and she said 'Frankie' - she looked calm but I could see her hands gripping the arms of the chair - 'Frankie,' she says 'life is very short so I've come to tell you that I still love you because I've always loved you and if you've got time for me I want to be your friend.' Rehearsed speech, shaky delivery, but okay, you know. Well I had no words at all. The depth of emotion was . . . . She was in my arms, that's all, she was in my arms, and . . . well, she's been in 'em ever since . . . .

Last May, last May was when she died. I've left a space for my name on her stone. 'In Love, United' - that's what I'm having. Sounds like a football team, but I don't care. Best years of my life. Great happiness like that, there aren't words . . . . *[Frankie raises her glass]* To my darling, bless her heart. *[She drinks. Pats the nearest dog.]*

scabs

TERESA SAVAGE

IT WAS IN NINETEEN SEVENTY SEVEN I think. Nineteen seventy seven. I'd had my hair permed afro. I was reading Angela Davis and Kate Millet. I had this poster on my wall of this woman with her mouth wide open shouting 'oppose, confront, resist'. Living in a communal house, smoking dope, listening to lots of Janis Joplin. I liked her. We all did. We listened to her so often we knew all the words. She was so outrageous

I laugh

so free. We were trying to work out our feminism.
So, you remember what it was like.
What happened was, there was this really big industrial dispute in the North West of London, it was called Grunwicks. A lot of Bengali women worked there and they worked in this factory. It was a film processing factory and they got some atrocious wages I can't remember what it was about twenty eight pound a week or something. And at that time I was earning

I sigh, knowing that every week it all went on beer and henna and silver bangles

I was really young about twenty or something, and I was earning five thousand pounds a year myself, but they were earning a total pittance.

So, after much negotiation with this firm they went on an all out strike, all these Bengali women. And it was a strike that, I suppose, just caught the hearts of loads of people because they, well, it was very clear to see the injustice of it. These women who were immigrants, who had very little English, were just being put upon basically by a ruthless employer.

I stop, thinking of Paola, the Chilean woman who comes to clean my house every week.

So, it grew into a really big dispute in London, over quite a long period of time. And all these women were out on strike, and lots and lots and lots of people started going there to this factory to support it. Support them. And anyway, it sort of won the hearts of loads of feminists, you know, because it was seen as a women's strike.

We went there a lot. We used to get up at five o'clock in the morning every morning and go up there before work. That was the time they used to bring them in. The scabs that is. Scab labour. Breaking the strike and making it last for such a long time, hoping to break the women. And we used to get up early and go up there. We were real professionals.

The memory of my young self makes me smile.

We had big boots so that nobody trod on our feet, we spent ages polishing them. And we took off our earrings and got rid of anything incriminating in our pockets.

I laugh.

And off we went. We'd go up there, and there'd be thousands of people, thousands, all linking arms. And we'd all be standing there in the freezing cold, stamping our feet, blowing into frozen hands. Five o'clock in the morning. Waiting for them to try. To try to bring the scabs in the buses. We'd all start pushing. We wanted to get in front of the bus, to put ourselves between it and the gate, to hammer on the sides and kick the tyres.

Here I wonder, was I scared, full of bravado, feeling reckless ?

Some mornings we'd win and the scabs would be turned away and other mornings we wouldn't. And we'd all get pushed away by the police. Who were pretty, you know, after many many mornings of this, were pretty pissed off with the whole thing, and quite aggressive.

Anyway, one morning we were all up there and we were all linked arms and waiting and waiting. We were about ten people deep outside the gates, stamping our feet and blowing into frozen hands when suddenly we knew the bus was coming. We knew because the people who were further up could see it first and started shouting scabs, scabs, SCABS, SCABS... and their shouting sort of came down to us in waves, and then we saw the bus. We all start pushing to try and get across the gates. And we're pushing, and pushing. And all the women all around where I was were linking arms, and shouting and shouting. And we were all getting pulled along, gripping on with our arms, our precious boots scraping along the pavement. Sometimes our feet even left the ground, and we'd be hanging between the arms either side of us, kicking our legs like silly cartoon characters. We were pulled along without knowing what was happening.

I wonder at myself, wonder at the exertion of all my strength, wonder at my invincibility.

I'm screaming abuse, being pushed and squeezed and dragged along, my mouth, like everyone all around me always open, screaming, scabs, SCABS. Suddenly I'm pressed right up against the police. I'm in the front row, pressed right up against them, still holding on to the other women. But they start trying to push us back, holding on to each other too, straining forward. So there's this big battle going on with us all pushing one way, and the police linked arms pushing back against us. They're heaving one way and we're heaving the other. Our bodies are pressed right up against theirs. Their faces are pressed right up against ours.

Was I scared ? I don't remember feeling scared. Only crushed. And claustrophobic.

Anyway there's this big copper next to me, and he had his face pushed right up against mine, and he's breathing heavily into my ear, his arms linked to the next bloke. But somehow his arms are all around me. His stubbly chin is so close to my face.

Even now I feel revulsion, what if it rasped my cheek?

Suddenly he whispers, so softly into my ear, so gently, so quietly, but even in that racket he sounded so clear. He whispers, in this really sickly voice:

I've always wanted to fuck a lesbian.

And I sort of looked round at him, startled. And I looked at him, hard into his face, and he just looked blank. His face was innocent.

Did he really say that? Of course, I knew.

fashion statement

LISA BELLEAR

Raybocks and reebans
And jeans with holes
And photographic chemicals
That leave a pattern
Of blotched bleached
Benign dreams

Henna your hair
If you dare
The smell
Of leather

Give out energy
Strong powerful
Black women's energy

Look at those
Wudjella women
Wanting a piece of
My womanist energy

Fantasising fanatically
On how we are women
Are oppressed and in
Our oppression we are
United

Thanks tidda girl
My wudjella sister

For your thoughts
And love and whatever

But I'm in love
With my Koori community

I'm in love
With Black women

Henna your hair
If you dare . . . .

women's liberation

LISA BELLEAR

Talk to me about the feminist movement,
the gubba middleclass
hetero sexual revolution
way back in the seventies
when men wore tweed jackets with
leather elbows, and the women, well
I don't remember or maybe I just don't care
or can't relate.
Now what were those white women on about?
What type of neurosis was fashionable back then?
So maybe I was only a school kid; and kids, like women,
have got one thing that joins their schemata,
like we're not worth listening to,
and who wants to liberate women and children
what will happen in an egalitarian society
if the women and the kids start becoming complacent
in that they believe they should have rights
and economic independence,
and what would these middleclass kids and white women do
with liberation, with freedom, with choices of
do I stay with my man, do I fall in love with other
white middleclass women, and it wouldn't matter if
my new woman had kids or maybe even kids and dogs.
Yes I'm for the women's movement
I want to be free and wear dunlop tennis shoes.
And indigenous women, well surely, the liberation
of white women includes all women regardless . . . .
It doesn't? well that's not for me to deal with
I mean how could I, a white middleclass woman,
who is deciding how can I budget when my man won't

pay the school fees and the diner's card club simply
won't extend credit.
I don't even know if I'm capable
of understanding
Aborigines, in Victoria?
Aboriginal women, here, I've never seen one,
and if I did, what would I say,
damned if I'm going to feel guilty, for wanting something
better for me, for women in general, not just white
middleclass volvo driving, part time women's studies students.
Maybe I didn't think, maybe I thought women in general
meant, Aboriginal women, the Koori women in Victoria
Should I apologise
should I feel guilty
Maybe the solution is to sponsor
a child through world vision.
Yes that's probably best,
I feel like I could cope with that.
Look, I'd like to do something for our Aborigines
but I haven't even met one
and if I did I would say
all this business about Landrights, maybe I'm a bit
scared, what's it mean, that some day I'll wake up
and there will be this flag, what is it, you know
red, black and that yellow circle, staked out front
and then what, Okay I'm sorry, I feel guilt
is that what I should be shouting
from the top of the Rialto building
The women's movement saved me
maybe the 90s will be different.
I'm not sure what I mean, but I know that although
it's not just women's liberation that will free us
it's a beginning.

package my spirit

LISA BELLEAR

Package my spirit into Waterford crystal
Take me to the sea and pour your words of valour
Of liberation and freedom over and over and over

As the sea spirit is moved by the barrage of mendacity
The waves are now swells following the passage of time
You continue to deceive and lie at the edge
Over my spirit the waves of time are not impressed

Who can tell the miracle seers that what they worship
In their eagerness to redress their guilt
Is full of hurt and hate?

Only the sea can know
That the bringer of liberation
Is the bearer of insecurities
Of anger to her people
The indigenous people
Her indigenous mother

So she dances to the oppressors
She makes frenzied wild ignited love
To those of all races but her own

And as she talks
Of freedom
Of 'our people'
The sea spirit knows

We don't seek retribution
We don't want to destroy
The speaker of liberation
Don't be afraid
Don't keep running
From yourself and your people
You can still speak of freedom
Of inter-cultural understanding
But this time you will stand
Beside our ancestors
Our elders our children
And speak of a future

Does she hear
The sea whispers
'Is she the one
The one who has suffered
Hard and long
Is she the liberator
Or is she the oppressor?'

As the waves withdraw the crystal disperses
To other indigenous peoples throughout the world
And the sea and I smile knowing
All indigenous people will be free
When those who dance
With and for the oppressor
Will too come home.
Don't be afraid
Don't be afraid

p u t

LILLIAN PREDIC-YOKSICH

Stojim na zlatnoj obali.
Opora i tvrda, slonova kost
u meni
prelama u kaleidoskop
moja sećanja . . . .

O, gde sam to stigla!
Do zlatne crte, da li je želim
jer daljine moćno zovu
mojih predaka . . . ?

Kaplje reč u tišini.
O, gde sam to zašla
kad stopa nosi znak kraja
i nemože se dalje!?

O, gde sam to pošla
jer ono vučje u meni
nosi me gore, nosi me lakše . . . ?
A hoću preko zlatne crte.
Sve dalje i dublje u sebe,
do dna i dalje . . .
A da li se može
ispod kože, u mekanu dubinu

                nerva

patnjom, do dna i dublje . . . ?

the journey

I stand on a golden shore.
Tart and hard ivory
within me;
breaking into a kaleidoscope
my memories.

Oh, to where have I come!
To the golden line. What do I want?
Powerful is the pull
of my ancestors' journeyings . . . .

A word drops into silence.
Oh, where did I go astray,
when a footprint bears its own end
and there is nowhere to go.

Oh, from where did I set out,
for that wolfishness within me
is carrying me on, carrying me lightly . . . .
Yet I want to cross the golden line.
Further and deeper within me
to the very bottom and further.
Oh, can one skim
under one's skin, to the soft depth
              of nerves,
suffering, to the bottom and deeper still . . . .

Teško je, ali mami
ta zenica sebe u vrtlogu dubine,
što dalje, što mekše ...
Preko zlatne crte, dok boli i

                peče,

al'mora se tako u sebe,

                      do sebe ...

It is hard; this pupil
of self lures me into eddying depth,
further still, softer still . . .
over the golden line, in pain, burning,
but one has to journey within oneself,
                    to oneself . . . .

the houses of pleasure

ANNETTE BLONSKI

IMAGINE YOU ARE A CHILD standing on the deck of a vast ocean-going ship that has taken four weeks to limp its way across two oceans and past many continents. Fire has broken out on more than one occasion, the food has been inedible, and you've learnt to speak a new language in the time it has taken to sail from Genoa to Fremantle. It might be Italian, because your little friend is related to the crew. Maybe it is Russian because she is from Kiev or Minsk or perhaps Siberia. It could even be German because this ship may have survived the war and be on its last run before being dismantled and sold for scrap.

Your parents and their new shipboard companions have spent the time between bouts of sea-sickness gripped by anxiety and the ever-present memories of blood and loss and fear, by impatience to start a new life, or just simply the desire to see what this great southern land really looks like. It is at the end of the universe, the bottom of the world, as far from the theatre of war and death as you can possibly go.

Does this continent have any cities at all? Fremantle was only a tantalising glimpse before sailing into the Southern Ocean and the Great Australian Bight. They were warned these were dangerous seas, and so they are. Punishing, gruelling, fanned by powerful westerlies that blow without cessation. For the most part, your parents are just relieved at being able to stand upright without throwing up.

But it is the light you cannot escape and do not want to escape, a brilliant light that forces you to squint all the time, a light that bleaches the land and washes everything clean. Your skin burns but you don't care. Years later your high school art teacher will show you the work of the *plein air* artists who, she will say with pride, were among the first to capture this incandescence. You will look at the sensuous pale yellow and olive and blue images of the bush with bemusement. The colours have nowhere near the intensity you remember from these first days approaching the majestically parched coast. Even more perplexing will be your first sight of a painting of a place that will be your first home, a painting by Albert Tucker of victory girls and their male companions in the pallid, unhealthy colours of the brown-out and Australia at war, the same war that drove you and your parents out of Europe.

For now though, you are standing on the deck, starboard side, gripping the handrail tightly, as a pilot vessel leads the ship through the heads of Port Philip Bay. On either side is land, apparently empty, tempting you. The time of arrival is at hand. You stare straight ahead. The ship moves inexorably towards and then past the Mornington Peninsula. An hour is a very long time but, hazy at first, then becoming clearer, you see a knob of land. You appear to be heading straight for it. You are sailing alongside the coast as if you were being driven in a car along a highway. Faint outlines of houses can be seen in the distance and then you seem to turn a corner. The ship rounds Point Ormond.

Standing clear before you is a city. You are so close to the buildings you can almost touch them. Some stand out, drawing your gaze towards them. They are ornate, or stately, or just plain strange. You will never forget them. They are the buildings that signify the end of a journey and the beginning of another story, another life.

Those buildings, you will later discover, are the Palais de Danse, Luna Park, and the Victoria Hotel on the corner of Kerferd Road and The Esplanade, houses of pleasure and escape, for the thrill-seekers and acolytes of oblivion. Above all, you will discover that what you see is St Kilda.

Another story, another time. Two middle-aged women prepare coffee, strong coffee that gurgles away happily on the green and white Kooka stove in an ancient espresso machine that threatens to blow up and shatter the little kitchen to smithereens. Both women are overweight but they do not care. Being fat signifies well-being. It means they have food and plenty of it, particularly cakes, many cakes, every day if they want. They eat them delicately, wiping the icing from their lips.

One woman dresses with no regard for her appearance. Plain, unfussed, practical. No make-up. She can have lovers whenever she wants them and the men don't seem to notice whether she is a fashionplate or not, she says with a wave of her hand. The other wears brightly coloured chiffon scarves, tossed around her neck, and speaks with a throaty growl. She has a face like a Noh mask, white with pancake powder and a bright red gash for lips, a bit like the make-up favoured by women today who wear black clothes and sip macchiatos on the terraces in Acland Street. Her lover (that is what he is of course, but the child doesn't understand) has taken up painting. After years as a bookkeeper, a master of creative accounting, he has turned to other artistic pursuits, mostly landscapes, mostly of the beach where he takes his daily constitutional, just down the road from Neptune Street, just down from this small terrace house with its cool rooms and the smell of latkes and knadlech and inedible, indigestible chulent.

The woman with the white face fixes the child with her sharp eye and says: 'Well, madele? And what are you going to be when you grow up?' The child is flummoxed. She says the first thing that pops into her head. 'I'm going to be a writer.' The woman smiles, satisfied. Her own son is a painter who painted searing visions of poverty and oppression in pre-war Melbourne. Her husband had come to Australia on a mission: to find a home for the Jews so they could escape the apocalypse he knew was coming. The Kimberleys were empty, he thought. Make a fine place for a new homeland. And the woman of the white face and her son had stayed on. The woman shakes away the memory, pats the child on the head and returns to her coffee. There won't be any nurses or housewives in this family, not if she has anything to do with it.

It is the 1950s. The streets of St Kilda are filled with the sounds of many languages. A trickle before the war, now the proverbial flood of immigrants. Middle European intellectuals and artists mingle with Australians while they do their shopping. Eastern European Jews argue about politics and worry about business, eating food that reminds them of home. Except that they don't ever want to go home. This is their home, little Europe in the Antipodes, a place from where they tentatively explore the ways of these fair-haired, fair-skinned descendants of Ireland and England and Scotland. Then to come scurrying back to the protective embrace of their own kind before once again making forays into this strange new culture.

Their skills and their talents go unrecognised so they work as labourers in the textile factories and building industry. They make contact here with the cadres of the Communist Party, joining the Eureka Youth League or Zionist organisations. Some establish businesses that eventually make a few of them rich; honorary members of the ruling elite. Only honorary, mark you.

To the child in the fifties, these people seem ancient, relics of a prehistoric age, and it seems as if they have been here forever. But they are refugees and their prehistory is the Europe of the late 1930s. Some got out just in time. Others didn't quite make it, yet somehow survived the war: in camps, in the army, among the partisans, hidden behind a wall in the bathroom by a friend taking incredible risks, or just head down, hoping the knock on the door would never come. Their stomachs were constantly churning and even now some things are indigestible, as though the body retains a memory of the time when it had almost nothing but fear and couldn't take anything anyway. Some people died because they ate too much too soon, after years of starvation.

When they first arrived, they went to live in apartment buildings like Victory Mansions on the corner of Acland Street and The Esplanade. Then they bought the tiny terraces in Robe Street and Grey Street and Neptune Street, where the smell of their cooking mingled with the salt in the sea breeze sweeping away the heat even on the hottest February day. Finally, they moved away to the newly-affluent suburbs where no one walks in the streets after dark. Years later their children return to St Kilda to live in flats in Eildon Road, or eat brisket at the Scheherezade, or to exhibit their art in the galleries. Even their parents come back, every now and again, or even every weekend, back to St Kilda to stroll and chat.

Is this the St Kilda of the painting called Victory Girls? The child, now grown, studies it intently. She struggles to reconcile this nightmare vision of Tucker's with the place she knows, with its luminescence and the warm maternal embrace, the place of refuge. In this painting is Tucker's war, where the combat and killing were far away but here, at home, the struggle was for something else. She can see clearly here in this image what she only ever glimpsed as a child, this country's unease about its role in the world and its sense of identity. Yet it had seemed so profoundly solid, a wall against intruders, which meant herself. Though she may not recognise the place, she recognises the fear felt by a nation on shaky ground. She has experienced this fear once before as a bewildered innocent forced to flee because her death was needed to secure another nation's unity, or at least so it seemed to those who loathed her.

But the fear is different here; it has another texture. The painting is shocking, an image of displacement, a displacement triggered by anger and confusion. As Tucker's anonymous men enact the macabre embrace of soldier and victory girl, the myth of the digger, carrying with it the longing for a homogenous, masculine national identity, has been sullied forever. These could be American soldiers, or Australian. Either way, the comfortable unities of place have been overturned. What remains is an image of profound disgust. That disgust is borne by the women whose bodies face the viewer while the men in their uniforms are merely shadowy presences, merging into the brown-out. It is as though the appetite of sex eats away at the women's flesh till the bones are exposed and the skeleton of decay is revealed. The fear of them, the loathing. Laid out before the young girl, imprinted on the women's bodies, is the fragility of Australian manhood.

She stares at the painting. She sees once again the place she lived in, the place she would visit, and the women who made coffee in their terrace kitchen. What she sees in St Kilda is another place where a new identity was being forged. Here the women were survivors, often tough and unforgiving. Spines of steel. This place was their first stop in a long journey in a new country that had been mapped (imperfectly) before they came and will continue to be mapped by succeeding waves of refugees and visitors, each with different eyes and expectations. A perfect location for struggle and strife, surprisingly peaceful.

The two women in the kitchen are older too and have become more comfortable, an imperceptible change, a slow unwinding, like the curious release of a tightly-wound spring. At any moment it might fly away, propelled by the force that keeps it bound. But for the most part it is not released. It is well-behaved, under control. They can begin to mask the painful feelings of displacement they first experienced, their confusion about what could be considered home, having to start again after a life that seemed to have only just begun and was over just as abruptly. How many lives can one person stand?

And then she remembers, as she turns away from the painting. They would make jokes about their first years here. One remarked that she thought times must have been very bad when she first arrived because almost every woman in Australia seemed to be a prostitute. (Is that not what Tucker is saying? Aren't the victory girls, the girls of St Kilda, all prostitutes?) The woman with the face like a Noh mask lets out a roar of laughter as she recalls why she had thought this. So many of the Australian women smoked cigarettes while they walked down the street. That is why. In Europe, only prostitutes and young women hoping to shock their bourgeois families smoked on the street. She laughs again. She lives next door to a prostitute now, but who cares?

This is not the St Kilda of the painting, it is another St Kilda, a place to begin again, not a place where old dreams die. It is a place where you can strike a new identity, a place of pleasure, a place where memory is constantly renewed and stories revised, the emblem of a dream.

For now, you can go to the beach and still see a child standing on the shore with a little bucket in her hand. She will look around her to see her parents dozing with one eye open to see she comes to no harm. After all, this is St Kilda so you need to be a bit careful with a young girl. The family might be from Turkey or Cambodia or Latin America. They no longer fear the knock on the door in the middle of the night although, like the people who came here before them, they still wake up sweating and screaming with terror.

The child feels that she has arrived in paradise.

eins zwei drei

LINDA WESTE

(i)

When your strange stiff shoes felt the Sydney coast
the learning began.
Assimilation and the 'abc', through rote, repetition;
rewards for casting off
a foreigner's accent and clothes.

The culture travelled with you,
harboured like a stowaway in your trunk,
yet precious as a trinket,
folded in a corner of your handkerchief.

Thoughts snagged with apprehension,
the swelling conflict, hovering.
Opa saw it coming.
He smelt death in the air and planned this journey early.
A calculated exit, perhaps a privileged one:
you pinned hopes like gold stars to his shirt.
Fear steered your family across the Pacific,
salt-spray stung in their tears for home.

Fritz Johannes Klaus Leopold.
Family names, verboten
when the war reports came.
Anglicised. Legitimised.

Interned you were at fourteen,
as easy as eins zwei drei;

both your spirit and your vocal cords destined to be broken.
Opa too, in 'alien' garb,
a 'national security risk' in your suburban street.
Taken away; and the neighbours withdrew guardedly
in prejudice and fear,
their parted curtains simply rustled,
broke the silence of their stares.

(ii)

Childhood was mysterious, with family history
to reconstruct like a jigsaw puzzle;
a piece here, a piece there, but always some missing.
Scrabbling impatiently for each
I grazed my knees on the knowledge.

When Oma died, so much disappeared.
The trunk, the steamer stamps,
letters to the past; Oma's letters, linked
like her four black basalt elephants, trunk to tail.

It reassured Father, their private burial
in a shabby suitcase;
he hoped its place on the highest shelf
would discourage all but dust.
His immigrant legacy,
this emphasis on respectability and reproof,
Our past concealed like a shameful tattoo.

To no avail; school children still cried 'Hun' and 'Heil'
and sang, 'Hitler had only one brass ball,
Caesar had two very small,
Himmler had one very sim'lar . . . .'
The tune itself a favourite for the Marching Girls' Band
which practised opposite our house;
spotlights beaming, the ovals awash with white,
starkened in the whistle's call to stop.

141

The mind's niche has no padlocks;
keepsakes endure. Childhood memories
swell with sentiment.
Pride still bounces on Oma's knees:
*'Hoppe, hoppe Reiter, wenn er fällt dann schreit er,
tishoo, tishoo,* all fall down.'

Opa/Oma - Grandfather/Grandmother

continental drift

THESE MEN WOULD FOLLOW ME, holding out my native language at arm's length, their mouths twisted with distaste. They would point out it had no bones of its own in its spineless body.
'Spoon!' I called back at them as if throwing salt, 'Spoon!'

'English,' he spat, 'English is the most lazy language, and so ugly!' I moved my mouth in contemplation of its sounds. Knowing myself that clarity is the last thing English ever asks of itself, that listeners will accept the vaguest approximations of vowel sounds and syntax, I acquiesced that, yes, there are more rigorous tongues. 'It is nothing; it just takes from all the others and calls itself English.'

'You are no problem for me,' he stated emphatically. 'I know German, French, Greek and Latin languages; you are no problem.' I spent a week in the Alps with Swiss Germans. I heard the deep rumble of avalanches and realised: the Swiss had something to be scared of. I might have spoken but they wouldn't talk to me. He only said, when I begged for mercy and to talk a little, 'You know I won't speak English. If your Italian improves then we can speak in Italian. I need to practise my Italian.'

When I returned to Spain I fell in love with my Spanish teacher. 'I am taking off my clothes,' I advised in Castilian, being careful with plurals and gender. 'I am taking off your clothes. You are taking off my clothes. You are taking off your clothes. We are taking off our clothes.'

Feeling tender, I thought of how he had loved me. Feeling sad, I recalled the note he wrote, man to man, to the friend who'd lent us his bed: 'Thanks for everything. I owe you a meal and a half.' It was written in Spanish. I wondered if I could share the joke. When he spoke English I did not love him as much. He lost the larger-than-life exaggeration lent by physical gesture and widening of the eyes; his face became paralysed, his hands tied. There is romance in language, I believed that . . . .

No language even compares, they will tell you in Greece, to Greek. 'If you learn Greek, you will relearn ninety percent of English,' he predicted. It is the father of all European languages; pure, potent and ancient. It is the father of Western civilisation. O pateras, oh paternal benefactor, o long long line of patriarchs nodding and blowing in each other's ears. It is the language where there is only ever one way to make a sound; with the mouth like so, and without questions because there are only answers. The first word in my new vocabulary was *exo*, outside.

I fell in love with a Greek man old enough to be my father. We sat in silence for hours, nights and nights across the marble benchtop in his kitchen, drinking and smoking. We would watch the moon moving behind the clouds from the patio. Confusion ran like a noise behind our voices. Sometimes I could glimpse the outline of a face or of a figure running in the shadows of our conversation; sometimes I sensed a form. When our relationship ended he answered enquiries from the curious with certainty: 'We had a philosophical disagreement.' He said, so he said.

This one from England I listened to carefully because he knew a thing or two about English: 'Even as a Latinophile, it remains plain to me, in this case, that the strongest and most resonant of English words and sounds hark back to their Anglo-Saxon roots.'
'Anglo-Celtic,' I corrected.
'That link has not yet been proven,' he said.
As he crowed out on the purity of Anglo-Saxon, I resumed my silence.

I returned to a place called home. My vocabulary had dwindled to its own dialect: English for foreigners; simple and direct. My speech enunciated its difference. One of my friends couldn't get past the accent. Its lilt distracted him like the incantation of a once known song. He looked at me with distance as he strained to hear my stories from the unknown, realising he no longer knew who I was. The ground was shifting. Focusing on my momentary advantage, I dream: his island drifts from my continent and he disappears quietly over the horizon.

like a banshee wail

LUCY JEAN MROZIK

I THINK OF ROS ALL THE TIME, wondering if they caught her, who she's bullshitting now. I know most of what happened at St Edmunds Street. I was there and all the rest, what went on in her head, I put together from her letters.

She'd leave me one day, I always knew that, but I didn't think she'd leave Karl Marx. He's her cat, a great neutered slob, the only living creature apart from me who's noticed . . . . He sleeps on her doona all day, waiting.

I lie there too, going over that morning.

'Soft dove pink,' she says. 'Can't you hear it?' She stretches and scratches her spiky hair. 'Ah,' she sighs, 'they're so gentle, they're washing Zarathustra away, washing away the faded edges of my dream.' Ros is like that, funny.

Often I'd say, 'That's crap, you're crazy', but now I remember things she said. Sometimes the words won't get out of my head, like music, you know, when it keeps going over and over.

It started early in the night. It's dark outside, but it's summer and she throws the window open, calls out, 'Hi! Where you off to?' to strangers passing by. All the noise from Chapel Street comes in and stirs her up. She rocks around the room and says things like 'God, can't you hear the pulse of life out there? It's driving me wild!' Half fooling of course, carrying on like a loony. She's gorgeous but she won't stop, goes on and on until it drives me mad and I kiss her on the mouth to shut her up. She pushes herself away from me, screams, 'Get out!' Wants me to leave her with her ideas. Yells that she has to get them down for posterity. She's talking so fast that I can't get a word in. I say 'Yer up yerself, Ros', and I get out of there.

Somebody's bought a cask of red. There's a guy there who moved into a corner of the lounge two weeks ago. He asks me if I know whose flat it is. He's a neat guy, has the corner set up like home, empties all tidy in a row. On a chair he's set up an altar with a picture of Jesus.

I go back in a few times to check Ros out but she doesn't even notice me. She's gone somewhere else, astral travelling she calls it. All through the night Ros writes like she's in a frenzy to get her ideas down on paper, or belts out stuff on the piano. I look over her shoulder at one stage and it's Beethoven. Ros is clever, really clever. Out of this world. She doesn't even know who's in her sitting room, getting blind on red. Ros doesn't touch it. Some woman I haven't seen before says, 'Why don't we shut that bitch up, doesn't she know about Craig?' Someone snaps at her, 'It's Ros you idiot,' and she says, 'So! And who is this Ros?'

No one really knows.

We're pretty low because Simon's just come over and told us that Craig's OD'd and we're all thinking it's rotten luck. Mostly we talk about music and dole queues or who's having it off with who, but after that we just sit and mope while Simon pulls at half-hearted chords on his guitar. Craig was a whiz on the guitar. Someone finds a birthday candle and lights it in front of Jesus, for Craig. We all bow down with our heads on the floor, say 'Om', and start to piss ourselves laughing. The guy who owns Jesus doesn't get up, just rolls over on his side and snores.

I sneak in to see if Ros feels like bed but she leans back in her chair laughing, butts out a cigarette in a pile of stubs. 'Listen to this,' she says and goes on and on until I fall asleep. I've still got the letter though. I found it screwed up on the floor when I took over her room.

She'd been writing to that poof. Poofters should be shot.

Dearest, dearest Andy Baby,
This time, I've got a fabulous idea, a collage made from collage! I'm going to call it 'Zarathustra', or maybe, 'The Eternal Recurrence'. Zarathustra and I have decided that the whole concept must be mathematically sound,

so I've incorporated Poincare's 'Recurrence Theorem'. That means of course that the sun, moon and earth must appear somewhere in it.

She carries on like this for about ten pages, there's a bit more about this Zarathustra and a whole heap of other crazy stuff. When Ros isn't writing or reading, she makes these amazing pictures out of anything she can get hold of. I've stuck them all up with Blu-tack. They glitter and change their colour when you move around the room and it's like she'll come running up the stairs, in a leather mini skirt and high heels, and say one of them's all wrong. She'll cut it all to pieces and yell that she's a failure and won't get out of bed for a week.

The letter goes on: *I've cut up a few of my collages, to express the fragmentation of my thoughts, as well as their continuity. I've arranged the little squares into the sun, moon and the earth. But above all, Andy-baby, I'm filled with a new love for humanity, so the picture must radiate all-consuming love. Life is wonderful!*

Also, I've cut off a small piece of my hair to show that even to mutilate oneself for love is not too extreme. (The clocks have all just changed time, Andy. Did you notice?) I'll glue this on the bottom right hand corner like a signature. My parents will go loopy. Mum will make me feel shit guilty when she sees the bald patch. Then she'll cry. Fuck my mother! Why does she have to look so sad? I'm so happy.
(The clocks have just changed again.)
I'm frightened, Andrew. I need someone to hold me safe all the time. Fuck fucking, I'm not interested. That's why I like being with you. Do you know who changed the clocks? I know this guy in Sweden I met once, he might know.

That page is all dog-eared. I read it all the time. I wish I'd known then. If Ros'd come back, I'd hold her. I didn't know. But then Ros didn't write letters to me. I'm not a poof. She goes right off in the last few pages, but then, in a way it all makes sense if you know Ros.

I planned my last essay while I jotted down some interesting variations to Scarlatti. Any nerd can follow Nietzsche's ravings. My essay was easy, easy, easy! I tell you Andy, it was brilliant! I'm not even bothering to hand it in, they know where to find me if they want it. I'm sick of being at everyone's beck and call. I think I'll incorporate the planets and stars in my collage, Andrew! The whole universe! Have just had another superb idea for a composition which would complement it. They're all pissed in the

lounge so I can try it without waking them up. I can't sleep anyway with this idea of combining Nietzsche and Poincare battering around in my head. Seeya. Must rush before I lose it.
                Ros-baby
P.S.   Who did change the clocks?
P.P.S.   I have got an even better idea for 'the sun'. It will be a mobile, the composition will have to wait. Brilliant!

Ros screws the letter up and throws it to the floor. Karl Marx's tail twitches when she starts belting out something new on the piano. I flop down beside him and watch her fingers going crazy on the keys. Karl leaps off the doona and streaks out to sit on the balcony, with the beer bottles. Somebody thumps on the wall of the flat next door. You can see Ros stop for a second and then try to go on, but she's lost her concentration. She's forgotten what she's doing.

She jumps up from the piano and starts pacing backwards and forwards as if there are too many things going on in her head and she can't find the one she wants. Blows smoke all around the place, sticking out her bottom lip so it'll shoot up and make the things spiral round that she's got hanging from the ceiling. Then she shoves her head out the window and screams, 'Shit, shit, shit, Zarathustra! Zara-a-a!' Drawing out the last 'a' like a banshee wail. I put the doona over my head and don't want to know. The thumping on the wall begins again.

Well, Zara must have come because, suddenly she sweeps everything off the desk, black stockings, letters, earrings, a few Big M cartons, and burrows until she finds whatever she's looking for. Reads for a while and then starts to write again so fast that it makes her earlier scribble like slow motion. She's forgotten about the piano and Andy-baby's letter is under her feet.

Every now and then she leans back in her chair and lights another cigarette before she reads aloud what she has written. She lets out a belly laugh that makes me want to grab her and hug her to bits but I know it's no use because she goes on writing, going so fast that you can hardly read what she has written. She's looking buggered, it's like there's a machine working inside her head and no one can find the switch to shut it down.

Ros falls on the bed beside me just before dawn. By the time it's getting light she's rabbiting on about the universe and doves. Then she's out of bed and bent over her desk writing again. I get up and take a look over her shoulder. It's to some guy Gavin I've never heard of. Half of it seems to be in some other language but you never know with Ros, she probably just made it up.

Suddenly she screws up the letter and throws it on the floor with the others. 'Karle-e!' she screams, 'help me!' And you can hear bodies stir. She runs out through the lounge as though the ideas in the bedroom were scaring her. Some guy murmurs, 'Fuck off'. She gets Karly from the balcony and sits on the bed sobbing, rocking him like a baby, her face buried in grey fur. Gradually she calms down. The cat gets fed up and twists in a flying leap out of her arms.

She jumps up quickly as though she's made up her mind about something. Perhaps it's because I've read her letter, perhaps I'm seeing things that aren't there but anyway, she's smiling, a hard glittery smile and hacking at the neck-line of the black t-shirt she's wearing. She cuts it up in a big lop-sided scoop and giggles a bit at her reflection in the mirror. It's as if I'm not there.

Starting at her forehead, Ros spreads lipstick over her whole face, and her big eyes stick out like she's wearing a kid's birthday mask. Tips out a packet of silver glitter and pats it over the surface of the red. She takes her time trying on earrings, and chooses big sparkling drops that nearly reach her shoulders. She looks in the mirror as though that's it.

I want to call, 'Hey Ros! What's going on?' and stop her, give her a shake, but she isn't Ros anymore; it's as though I'm watching her through a telescope, a bright glittery star going on some journey I can't follow. So I don't try to stop her when she drifts out, wearing her latest ideas like a fancy dress, down the stairs and into St Edmunds Street.

transfer fee

You don't disport, but drift
into the music's end of the century
its enchanted whine
beneath the pillared encyclopaedia chandelier, fobbing off his serious
'I mean' she says 'your doe eyes make me puke
and crisp hosannas shouldering their pasts'
Once-pretty boy bats on till stumps, plastered through his phase
while Unobstructed chomps
'I really liked you but' she says
and lies could grow together, like welded
Friends tickle and the room's got dirt on it
Why don't they disappear. posthumous, mutinous
tearjerking to last week's binge or fruit
'Tell the big deal crumbs I never. Why don't you swim in that?'
Mummified, unreal, the party's swoons across river'd air
as each new toy or shadow rocks

memoir

GIG RYAN

Seeing him again is nothing, if it ever was
Hope and matelessness jingle together
He starts a smokey wound
Things then were oblivious
Time was panic stations
The bed's mock sun presumed a wedding
brambles and delay
He could surely guess the aberration that you were
as now beneath a vane of light
hollow and sullied
you unpick birth's one true foreign bassinet
A paraclete with a plastic flower and torch

album

you thought it might be worth trying. better than being sent to the kookas again for taking part in the riots. you were fortunate to be one of the twenty chosen to participate in the pilot scheme of the album plan. most other troublers still had to do their time in the k's, but anything was better than being locked up in a dark room, crackling with loud laughter, for ten hours at a time. it made you feel lilliputian. the continued assault of laughter attacking from invisible ducts in quadrophonic sound made you shake and cry. you found it impossible to regain your sense of humour when you were released. although you were determined that the kookas would never stifle your intentions to keep protesting against government philosophy. there would always be those who would make public their disapproval of the debt levy. why should the provident and the poor have to be penalised, some forced to exist on rations, because of others' profligate ways. still, you decided to join the album plan because it sounded less of an ordeal than the k's. it would give your nerves a rest.

four times a day, every six hours, it would summon you with its simulated bell call, not unlike church bells you occasionally heard in old movies. it was quite beautiful, a carillon they used to call it. you checked it on the encyclopaedisc. after the first few days you were always ready at least five minutes before you were required to lens line-up. your hair neatly brushed high back from your forehead. face freshly shaved. teeth cleaned. the tv turned down, the visible parts of your apartment dusted and straightened up. then you would calmly pose in one of the ten suggested positions to have your portrait, your condition recorded by the tiny pink video camera installed in your living quarters. nothing hidden about it. it was there right there for you to see. pearly pink. cyclopina 111 was its official name. you had come to realise how lucky you were to have been chosen for this trial scheme. this self assessment program. in fact you were enjoying the whole procedure. you'd been fascinated by your own image for a long time. even when you took your first steps at ten months they were towards a full length mirror. when your image appeared immediately on the screen below the lens you were required to key in your report on any changes in your facial expressions. any negativity, any hints of anti-social feelings were to be observed and commented on. this way it was felt individuals could share, contribute to their rehabilitation. it was a way to divert useless social resentments and rebellions. to discard them like old skins. they did nothing to enhance your physical appearance. they made one look troubled, wrinkled, aged. with lips tight, twisted. forehead red and frowning. the program had been designed so that at the end of one month subjects who had displayed excellent self awareness and self monitoring skills: noticing, commenting on every facial mood, category inventoried on the central grid at the state psychobank, would be emancipated from their felon tag and given the opportunity to promote and exemplify the benefits of the album scheme. as a member of the narcissus team you would be able to give lectures on tv and tour both urban and rural precincts giving witness to your personal transformation. you would play a video documentary of your changed, more salubrious countenance. not just quick before and after images. something much more thorough. you would be allowed to edit the film, choose the best shots. you would even be allowed to draft your own script from your original reports.

posters of your testimonial would be displayed in public places. you would became a celebrity, promoting the virtues of the album scheme of self knowledge to the general population. you would knock on doors. insist on people's responses. you would recommend they agree to cyclopina (it wasn't mandatory) once a month, the equipment being installed free of charge. you would explain the range of recording postures available to them. you were to report anyone showing hostility to the scheme. they would be close-uped by needle cam, recently inserted in every road gate of the state. and because you would be making such a contribution to society you would be able to join the ranks of those who had already received life long exemptions from the debt levy.

ANNA GIBBS

terminal

THE SCREEN FLICKERS. THE reflection flutters across your face, empties the colour from your eyes. You stare as if transfixed. You're ready for take off, starting down the runway, moving through the letters of the logo, flying now ... somewhere out there in digital space ....

From the plane coming in to land, the new city looks gift-wrapped: a tangle of over- and underpasses round a cluster of buildings. You sense the promise of arcane knowledge: you don't just enter this city; you must be initiated into its mysteries. And by them, transformed.

Instead of magic you find work. Spend your time trying to stitch together something that will bind you to this new place, even temporarily, but you're working in elastic, suspended in a placeless space. You dream you're a fugitive, trying to parachute to safety from a plane that's about to explode, find yourself bungie-jumping instead, attached to a spiralling telephone line, flung out over a void, subject to sudden returns in which you crash-land in the broken fragments of another life.

Out of the past comes the smell of burning. Flaming bridges collapse and sink into soundless canyons. Over and over the image repeats on your private screen. She's a real loop, they say at work.

When you get home at night the call comes, disguising its voice to lure you back into narrative, the same old story. Each time the phone rings you think, I won't answer that, but you can't stop yourself, you can't stop and before you know it you can see your own hand lifting the receiver in spite of your best intentions and suddenly you're back in character even as you hear the voice say, sarcastically, *that's uncharacteristic, for you not to answer the phone straight away. Usually I can tell, you're waiting for my call, sitting hunched over the phone and I can tell because you always lift the receiver on the first ring.* And the voice is right, although sometimes you've managed to hold off for the second or even the third ring, simulating breathlessness as you speak - and then some wrong number at the other end takes this as a sign of your willingness to engage, for a price, in nameless practices.

You leave the voice and go back to bed. Turn on the VCR and watch the series on border crossings: The Great Wall of China, the Rhine, the Rio Grande, the Pyrenees, the Andes, the St Laurence Seaway, the English Channel, the Berlin Wall. Backwards and forwards the cameras pass, crossing and recrossing boundaries in every conceivable mode of transport, as if, it seems to you now, the more ancient and uncomfortable the vehicle the better the crossing can be constructed as transgression. Having crossed a line everything will change, by virtue of that act alone. You can feel the anxiety in the face of collapsing boundaries, the disappearance of distance. You snuggle deeper in place under the doona.

By day, planted in the terminal garden, fingers rippling over the keyboard, you go wandering. Now it's Tokyo, city of signs. Night at 4.30 pm. You make your way through the calligraphic streets, an illuminated manuscript of incessant, raving neon. Not far from Shibuya Station in the only remaining dark pool of sky you see the letters SEED, powder blue, apparently unattached to anything, enigmatic, like a message of promise. A new nature. Inside the grey integument of the pod, the 'Next Life Interior', they're selling crystals as big as boulders at the Gaia counter on the SeedGate floor and above, on Proto, Composition and beyond, avantgarde designer clothing. You see the possibility of your chrysalis body transformed, translated into the idioms of the corporate authors: Issey Miyake, Kenzo Abe, Comme des

Garcons - and re-emerging in other lives, a succession of ephemeral works. The images whisper, more among themselves than to you, the eavesdropper, intrigued. *Zawa-zawa oto ga suru,* you remind yourself for practice, just under the beat. And you pass out of the mouth of desire into an atmosphere something like air. On the wall outside there is a huge billboard with an image of a whale disappearing into a vast ocean. I'm here, it says. I'm glad you're there. You turn down the tiny street alongside Wave and Loft where a somewhat shrunken Godzilla prowls the alleys, soliciting for the cinema, the seventeenth sequel. Pedestrians sweep by without a glance at the *gaijin:* you could have worn your pyjamas and it wouldn't have mattered. No need of passports beyond the access code today . . . . Time disappears week after week in the Tokyo layout.

You forget to eat, lose the taste for food. Sometimes out of habit, or as if sleepwalking, you open the fridge door in the night and stand mesmerised in the luminescent glow that fills the empty shelves, spills out to catch the gleaming white goods, pale presences whose electric hum haunts your pacing through the flat. You dream to the rhythms of the fridge, which purrs contented as a cat as it mainlines from the socket: supply supply supply.

Suchard Lindt Droste Guylian Red Tulip Cluizel Perrugina Ferrero Rocher Tobler Anthon Berg Holfbauer Duc d'Or Dolci d'Oro Godiva

You scan a story about Australian tourists in the US: they're on a bus trip through the Grand Canyon and the driver says, s'pose you Aussies are going to tell me you got a bigger one back home. No, they say, but we've got a rock big enough to fill it.

In search of a rock of your own you return to the old place after almost a year, drive back to your abandoned flat at the top of a crumbling colonial mansion. Two months after you left, the house was sold and the other tenants were given notice. One of your friends had written to you: 'I kept driving past your old flat expecting to see your light on and your shadow on the blinds. Well in the end I broke in to prove to myself that an era was over. I walked round and round the rooms, remembering old times. The place was so quiet. I feel strange confessing to you now. But I've started to tell you, and you might as well know all. I found an old cassette and put it on my walkman just to shut out the silence; it was from your answering machine - all those other absences of yours coming back to haunt me through the headphones . . . . '

So now you go back too, just as a tourist, to survey the sights. But when you round the corner you see the old wooden staircase to your front door has been torn away and the entrance bricked up. The way back is sealed off: the fantasy of return had been your own. You're in shock and memory forecloses. Go to Beaufort Street, some one says, and you think, Beaufort Street . . . Beaufort Street . . . .

The roads that take you backwards are never the ones you look for. It's like looking at a mirage: you focus to see it better and it disappears.

Back in the other place, you plan ordered itineraries for other travellers. You live like a ghost in the megalopolis where time passes without you noticing, where days stretch to suit your inclinations and night never falls unless you give the command. The world miniaturised for the palm of your hand is not a globe but a disk. You no longer unfold enormous maps on the floor and fight with the cat to read them. You inhabit the terminal garden - a field of screens blooming under fluorescent light - and lose yourself in the pixel cityscape while Similar the corrugated cat sleeps on the VCR, lifts his head at the sounds of wildlife, stretches and falls back to convulsive sleep, dreams of chasing rabbits.

The screen flickers like a moth and the answering machine records the voices.
So that's your game. You knew it would be me calling and that's why you've put the machine on. It's 4 am where you are, so I know you're home. Well dream on, then, but remember, reality catches up wth you in the end.
You don't pick up the receiver.

In the night you wake from a dream, you were in Tokyo, the research trip for the layout, and you emerge from the cinema in Shinjuku to realise you'd been sitting in the very building you had just witnessed Godzilla trample.

The feeling of disbelief - the city is still there, you are still alive - hangs about you like an aura. Too amazed to trust yourself to sleep, you turn on the television. On a WWII documentary bodies are being bulldozed into mass graves; on the next channel an inert body seems to have delegated its vital signs to a wall of monitors while a team of white coats and plastic gloves refits it with spare parts. Deeper into the night the screenlike faces of soap opera stars pass and repass. Repetition renders them soundless. Movement flashes without effort from edit to edit. Sometimes you forget all volition, and lie motionless as the voices on the answering machine land like planes on a distant tarmac, origin unknown.

I know you're there. You're not at work, I've just checked. You're crouched on the lino in the corner of the kitchen and you're listening to my voice coming out of the machine. You're paralysed. You couldn't pick up the receiver now even if you wanted to. You can't interrupt me. You're too curious about what I'm going to say - what I'll be free to say now I don't have to talk to you personally. Now I can invent you.... Perhaps you think I'll ask you to call me back. Perhaps you think I'll leave the next move to you. So you can not call me back. But I'm not giving you that option. I'm not leaving a message.

And in the middle of the night, your analyst, trying his own version of shock therapy, delivers lines from a movie even worse than the one you remake night after night, deep in the REM state.
You're on the line. Right now is all that matters. Everything else is history. Speak now or forever hold it. You can trust me but you have to tell me everything. Everything do you hear? Speak now.... But you're already rigid, as if electrocuted. Your hair - an electric red mistake - stands upright; looks like you do it with your finger in the socket, someone tells you. Brains are fried. Microwaved - cooked insides, you overhear later.

You close the fridge door again, leave it to the sounds of its own satisfaction. Get in the car and head back home to the source. Arrive in Adelaide two days later and your mother puts you in your old room, a museum of a sixties childhood.

In this house you learnt the politics of space; came to understand the concepts of border and frontier, the relative strengths of tactic and strategy. You found out for yourself the meanings of sabotage and guerilla action as Australian and American troops were defeated in the flickering blue light of the lounge room.

The house was a territory, increasingly finely demarcated, though the boundaries were drawn in invisible ink and only the heat of the moment made them suddenly legible before they cooled back into banality. Life disappeared down the sink - or left by the window as you did at night when the gully breezes called you into the foothills. Sometimes, when you returned in the morning you found everything in your room thrown into an angry pile in the middle of the floor, drawers and cupboards gaping, the bedspread rucked up to expose the emptiness beneath. It was your mother's house, as she reminded you and your sisters - and while you remained, there were rules.

You were eating her alive.

You retreated to your room at the end of the passage. You moved your bed so it lay facing the door. You wedged yourself into the space between, back against the door, feet bracing the bed. Here you could sit for hours, pouring over the atlas, wishing yourself elsewhere, holding your small space against all incursions.

Now, though, you pace the streets, searching for something lost. If anyone asked you, you couldn't say what.

Crossing King William Street you see a headline about the Beaumont children; after all these years, still the same news. Every time you go back they're draining another pond, consulting the clairvoyants, finding fresh evidence. A suitcase full of newspaper clippings on a rubbish tip seemed to promise revelation. It turned out to be an old lady's hobby. The whole population is obsessed with the story.

Mostly, children went missing in other ways. Lacking an international airport, refugees from family life fled to the east coast and Sydney, Sin City. You never even met a Catholic till you went to Melbourne. It feels so much more wicked to make love with your clothes on, one of them whispered to you in a dark corner of some conference dance before you lost your head.

It seems to you now that this city is shrinking, although its centre is filled with multi-storey carparks - car motels, modular capsules from which white light leaks at night, catching at the edges of cavernous holes where buildings used to be. In the skyscrapers floor after floor of empty office space is measured in acres while the suburbs gasp for air. Caught in a corridor between the hills and the sea, they expand lengthways down a narrow belt of land. The names of the beaches at the far ends of the coastal strip were once unfamiliar and exotic: Noarlunga, Willunga, Moana. You remember Willunga full of almond blossoms, and Moana as a beach covered in thick matted seaweed. Inland, on the furthest outskirts, Elizabeth and Salisbury were satellite cities, as far away as the moon.

The nightly weather report still divides the state into settled areas and vaster spaces termed 'unsettled areas'. Settled, then, meant safely subdivided; a land tamed and mapped, gridded to fit the street directory, neat rows of quarter acre blocks. To settle was to stay put: to build a house, to erect fences, to keep people out. Home ownership and private property.

Now you notice that everyone in town drives just below the speed limit and a man who rides his bike past you on the footpath one hot night calls out excuse me as he goes. But round the intimate dinner tables lit against surrounding night, the stories still circulate: the gay academic drowned in the river by persons unknown; the bodies of young boys found in a restaurant freezer; the Truro graves of missing girls. Sex and death are linked in the city's lexicon. Good manners settle like suffocating pillows over sleeping faces. Breathing subsides; the slow currents of the unsaid travel down the spacious streets on summer nights, seep out through the parklands surrounding the CBD, eery deserts of dried grass studded with trees.

The raucous seventies have long since left town. Those were the days when young men destined to become state and federal politicians went to parties in lesbian households, where ex-wives lived, and helped their mates shoot up in the toilets. Dykes took over the Festival Centre and landed jobs on the minister's staff. Maintain your rage, the population was exhorted. These days there could be valium in the water supply.

You leave again the day you get the crossed line.

Is that you? What's all that garbage on the line? Look, he keeps on calling me. Five or six times a day and I just don't know what to do any more. I've perfected the art of imitating an answering machine but I'm sure he knows. I say hello, then he begins to talk and I recognise his voice, so I say 'I'm sorry I'm not at home at the moment but if you'd like to leave a message just give your name and number and I'll call you back as soon as I can.' And then I go 'eep' just like the beep you get. But he never says anything, he just hangs up. I think maybe he does think it's a machine though . . . .

You drive aimlessly from town to town and all you can think is that you're travelling through the driest state in the driest continent in the world. You stop for a drink, then pick up a pair of teenage hitch-hikers for their safety and your sanity. You're a real cool dude, they tell you by way of thanks. Then, after a longish silence: are you a boy or a girl? What's the difference? you say. Get real, they tell you.

Dior Chanel Country Road Schiaparelli Sportscraft Issey Miyake Carla Zampatti Gucchi Yves St Laurent

You scan the airwaves, searching for the sound of the human voice. The whole landscape is criss-crossed with talkback, a city of the air floating beyond the ruled boundaries of the built up areas. Can anyone tell me what year metric was introduced in Australia? someone wants to know in this age of information. Sure, a different voice states with confidence, it was 1956. Five minutes, then someone rings in with a correction: No, he says, it was 1966. The breeze from the open window tears past your ear. Is this for real?

You call in to check your bearings.
Talk to me. Just talk to me. Please . . . . Your voice comes closer than you ever will. I know this is just a crazy fantasy but it feels like your voice is reaching out to touch the inside of my ear, only it's so intangible, this kind of touching and I keep wanting more. I want your voice to enter me and take me over. . . .

And for a moment you're back there with her, in the Willagee pub, protected and preserved, in air-con comfort, from whatever the world might be outside. The view you're offered is confusing: an image of plenitude in the midst of desolation; emptiness at the heart of a strange beauty. The scale is all wrong - whether too large or too small you couldn't say. What you can see: a strip of highway and a piece of scrubby land cleared of everything except a few bleak clumps of dessicated grass. A single outsize margarine container rotates at the top of a long pole so that the family gathered round the table smile vacantly out over the intersection while the lights change and the traffic moves on and they too pass like a royal wave to be replaced by a black and white cow grazing in pastures of unreal green, oblivious to the swoosh of semis below.

As unreal as cyberspace.

Tuning into another channel in search of some kind of connection you try matching your voice exactly to the one on the tape, bending the notes to reproduce faithfully the particular plangency of country and western - songs about faithlessness.

There's just one thing different
just one thing new -
I've got your picture
she's got you

Repetition and difference.

He gives me love
I never got from you
His love is true
Why can't he be you?

The triangulation of desire. It's object always already lost. The story of your life.

But there's some rewriting to be done, thresholds to cross as you travel through this particular plot-space, heading like a letter for another destination. Arrivals are incalculable events - accidents waiting to happen. You could be carried away on the slip of a tongue or returned to sender: WRONG WAY GO BACK. Take a risk, you tell yourself. Keep going; no one wants to be a dead letter.

And instead of a story, a kind of complication starts to take place. Traces of narrative, effects of reference, vestiges of character, turns and returns of phrase and image, detours, digressions and changes of gear: all these make a different geography where even as you leave you ceaselessly arrive. Just temporarily, when the terminal's hot, you could be coming or going, Arthur or Martha. Completely wired.

The switchboard lights up and the call comes.
I've been watching you. I know who you are.

You put it on hold and press the accelerator. You're on the road, heading for the deadline while all the time you know that something escapes you, something you're trying to say.

i, pronoun

JORDIE ALBISTON

I, the ninth letter and third vowel of the Roman alphabet, going back through the Greek *Iota* to the Semitic *Yod*, represents a consonant (= English *y* in *yearning, youth,* etc.); in its original sense, we can thereby surmise that I is equal to why, which being the initial consonant and question of you, yourself (as person, pronoun, ex-lover) only goes to show that we share a connection after all. You, used with no definite meaning as indirect object, or (better) qualified by a preceding adjective (as in *cruel, uncaring*) and I, as substantive, or *metaphorically* the subject or object of self-consciousness, no longer adhere to such a connection. For I, being connective or quasi-connective L. -*i*-, being the stem-vowel, as in *beauti-ful*, or a weakened representative thereof, as in *carni-vorous*, can no longer vow that forming plurals of Y(ou) and I, as in the phrase *yours faithfully*, is possible. I, as a pronoun by which I denote myself, in the nominative case, am not to be henceforth referred to as half or any part therein of the word *us*, a term no longer in use. Examples in English of such grammatical independence could be *I am alone*, or a strengthened representative thereof, as in *I am strong*. Any deviations of the oblique cases of the singular outlined above can only lead to misuse and abuse of I, as in *me*.

as blind as a blue sky in australia

ANGELA SEWARD

'It often happens that just before an understanding of some matter there is a stage of denial, or blindness, or deliberate not seeing, just as the sea withdraws from the sand before throwing forward the thundering wave.'

The Australian said the sky was blue where she came from.
 I said of course the sky is blue. The sky is blue everywhere, that is in the nature of the atmosphere, that is in the nature of light.
 She said yes, that was true but no blue was the same. She said that I would not understand what blue she had in mind. She said the sky where she came from was not this blue I knew, this blue like a thin wash. She said the blue she knew and remembered was like the blue of Yves Klein.
 That blue I certainly do not know. A sky like that I will have to see to believe. A blue like that will be bluer than the blue of the Midi. I do not, however, think that the Australian ever lied to me.

Sometimes I lie in my bed and dream. Sometimes I dream of ripping open the Australian's belly. I use a knife. Otherwise I give her my eyes on a plate, to let her do the looking.

One day I asked the Australian if she was from Sydney. She said she was not. She said she had never been to Sydney. I had to say that I did not know any other towns in her country and she said that this was no surprise. She said she came from the other side, from the other side of the continent. It sounded like a loss to her when she told me this, or perhaps it was the name of the town, which I forget now, that made me think about loss and this Australian with her mouth full of water and no tears in her eyes. She said it took a while to get from her town to Sydney and she looked at me for a moment and then she smiled. She said that perhaps a while in Australia was different from a while in France.

'We have only the world that we bring forth with others and only love helps us bring it forth.'

I said to the Australian why don't you marry me and we will go together and live in Sydney. She laughed a deep belly laugh that knew something I didn't know. That might be nice for you, my friend, she said, but as for me I will be nobody's wife.

    I suppose that the Australian will have it her way, under her blue sky. And she will put stars in her pockets that I will never see in my life. I do not think that the Australian ever lied to me, but I realised later that in her deep belly laugh there was a pain opening like the black slit of a mountain crevasse, a pain so profound she would never fathom it. The slit had closed over at the end of the sentence, but later, when it occurred to me what I had witnessed, I wondered whether, in her wifelessness, the Australian would ever come to know herself. And I could not help but remember that pain which rarely saw the light of day and wonder what events . . . .

When I reflected upon the Australian in this manner I would always begin to feel as if I were committing a sin. For the Australian did not believe that there was a self. She said the concept was a Greek tragedy and no longer relevant. The Australian said that if there were anything like a self then it existed as bits and pieces of other things, fragments kaleidoscoping from multiple and diverse sites. She said belief in a unity could lead to a position that was essentialist. She said that depth was an outmoded and unuseful concept and that she preferred to exist in the shifting surfaces of things.

Sometimes I did not understand a word the Australian said.

She liked to talk about finding truths in the gaps between. I wondered whether she noticed the dull pain in her laugh. I wondered whether she would ever realize that gaps do not exist. I did not tell her about my wondering. I did not dare, for it would have been confessing another sin. And I certainly did not tell her that I did not believe in contradiction.

I told the Australian that I felt confused by the idea of not having a self. I asked her what I should call this feeling of being whole, of being alive with pleasure in my bones and in my flesh, this feeling of being someone where once there was no-one. I asked her if she had never been dead. I asked her if she had never been lost. I asked her if she had never felt some part of her self was missing. I said to the Australian look at me I am my self where once I was not. I said to the Australian this is something that I know.

The Australian laughed at me when I spoke to her like this. She said you do not understand theory, don't you see? You do not understand how language brings you forth, and me.

I said I understand very well when I am speaking my self and when I am being spoken by someone else. I said this is not a question of degree, this is a question of place. I said do not argue with me!

This was how the Australian and I would begin to fight.

She would say you are a materialist. I would say it is all very well to label me but what is important is whether I am received.

She would say Roger, over and out. The Australian had a way with words. It forced me into corners.

I shouted at her well the sky is blue isn't it?

She would say yes of course the sky is blue because that's the way we humans see it but the sky is many things, a mixture of gases for instance, and the blue, well the blue is an absence of other colours, an absence of other wavelengths. She would say look there's no point me speaking to you, you won't listen. Forget it. I don't want to fight.

I said to the Australian I want to go where your blue sky ends and when I get there I will kill you off. There will be no more arguments then.

Go on then, she said, Go! See if I care!

You don't care about anything, I said.

The Australian paused. The Australian looked at the floor. She said well I don't care about you, not the way you want me to. When she said it, it always stung my face and my heart would crease. What kind of world is this, I'd think, and then I'd wish I could be Pol Pot and get rid of all the intellectuals. Get rid of her, at least.

You force me to say it, every time, she said. Over and over again. The same bloody scenario.

I'd take her out into the countryside, to the bank of an irrigation canal. I wouldn't bother with a blindfold. I'd put the barrel of the pistol to her temple as if I were a South Vietnamese General and I'd pull the trigger. A matter of fact. Her legs would crumple beneath her torso and she'd pitch down the slope into the shallow water. I'd cut off all her hair and break her legs. Her blood would glisten on the brown earth until it dried. Her blood would stain the water like ink stains, crimson where it poured out of the head - a stream within a stream turning a pale and paler pink as it spread along the ditch. Her blood would irrigate the land. Let the wild boars eat her flesh, let them break their teeth on her bones.

Into the silence of my imagining she said you ask for it you know.

Being as angry as this made me want to cry. I'd bite the inside of my bottom lip to stop the truth from surfacing. The Australian never forgave a public display of hurt. She said that if men cry it means that they are capable of feeling. She said that if women cry it only shows they are weak and in need of protection. And she was not going to be anyone's mother. If she wanted a child, she said, she would have had one.

I'd stare into the table top until she asked me what I was thinking. I'd tell her I was planning how to kill her.

And what did you do to me this time?

Shot you in the head.

I didn't tell her that I had broken her legs. I didn't tell her I didn't want to kill her.

Being as angry as this made me want to faint.

When you shot me in the head, she asked, was there a blue sky?

The Australian's neglect hit my chest again and again and the sobs dislodged themselves like thick green phlegm. I doubled over crying like a child coughing up a missing mother. If only the Australian's hand could have reached out to me then, if only the Australian could have touched my body, the back of my neck, the processes of my spine, if only the Australian could have crouched beside me with her head close to my breast and her hand in mine.

The Australian kept her distance. The Australian never apologized for anything. She would offer to make a cup of tea. A cup of coffee. An infusion of rosemary.

The Australian said why don't you write me a happy story.

What, with an ending and a blue sky?

If you like . . . whatever you like.

I do not come from your lucky country where the sun always shines and there's plenty of space.

Christ you're difficult, she said.

I do not think that the Australian ever lied to me.

On other occasions the Australian would simply leave. She would get to the door and say in a tight soft voice that she was not going to stay. Perhaps she went to a park and sat beneath a blue sky and dreamed of home. I do not know where she went when she wanted to avoid me. I do not know where the Australian is. In the beginning there is hope and then there is none.

The Australian used to say you make life hard on yourself, you are young and free, you should be out in the world doing things, you should be happy. The Australian said you are too hard on people, on me. I'm not perfect, you know.

Suddenly the Australian was leaving my country. There were signs for weeks before her departure but she did not tell me of her intentions and I did not see the signs because I wanted her to stay. The signs became a sentence hovering in my mind.

You are leaving, I said.

Yes.

This was how the Australian said goodbye. When I asked her to embrace me she complied.

The Australian's body felt like a limp animal, freshly slaughtered. Her body was neutral, neither giving nor taking, and I felt an embarrassed distaste for my needs in her mechanical arms. I felt a rage stick in my throat and I might have screamed it then:

What kind of country do you come from? What kind of people brought you forth? You strut about waving other people's theories as if they were a life to live! And you tell me to write happy stories with blue skies. Well, where are yours? You've got the heart of a corpse. You don't want to love, you want to donate. You'd rather steal a world others are only too happy to give, and then pretend they weren't there. Who taught you this negligence? Can't you see how your ignorance kills?

There is no point in speech when the answer is that you asked for it and it's a power struggle, didn't you know? There is no point in speech when the answers will be closed doors and exits. The Australian would have said the truth is difficult to face. I love you but I do not want you in the way you desire. You must go through this on your own. The Australian did not speak and neither did I. The Australian had a passport and an aeroplane ticket. The Australian left.

A long time afterwards I was in an art gallery looking at the canvases of Yves Klein and I began to think of the Australian and her blue sky. I remembered a story she had read to me and the first line:

'*I saw the spring come once and I won't forget it.*'

I looked at the blue of Klein and I saw with my eyes that the Australian must have lied. No sky could be that blue, I said aloud. Then I remembered how the story ended. I heard the Australian's voice and how she said

'*I thought my heart would break*'

as if she meant it.

from common knowledge

JAN MCKEMMISH

Sometimes I feel the heart go out of me.
Sometimes I feel the heart ripped out of me,
quite gently,
it is not pain,
just the absence.
I feel the heart go out of me,
I sigh. It comes back eventually.
I forget again, as I do every time.

She is having a cup of coffee and a cake. It is seven in the morning. She is sleepy and thinking familiar thoughts wearied by repetition in half sleep. These mornings, stealing coffee time from the boss or from herself. She sits with her cup and no resentment. It is silent in the cafe. A radio is on in the kitchen out the back, just in time for the news it is switched over to music. The cafe remains silent. She sips her coffee. Another, please. She is mechanical. Reaching for a cigarette. The day begins.

Some years exist only as a memory of great tiredness.

If I were to begin with a clean sheet of paper.
If I were to write as if for the first time.
I would record Monday night, sitting with Carol, nearly two years now and the cancer is escalating. She is strong.
And I would record my reluctance to do the requisite nursing. It is past midnight and I have to be at work at six. I live in the shift-work gloom and the terror of not sleeping.
She calls it a crisis but the language is not right. Crisis implies an urgency, that things are moving fast (which is true of this cancer), and also that something can be done, when I know it can't. I have been through this before with my father, though his decline was faster and

less gentle, less kind. Is dying ever kind? I am pessimistic and set against involvement. Only doing this because our mutual friend is out of the country and I am a substitute.

A Monday night, a steel calm after intravenous valium at two in the afternoon, newly capped teeth for me, like that, snap, and I am that calm through the difficult night, one you can never imagine until it occurs.

There is a relentlessness about it. We all wish to deny the imminence, now that it is here; will we recognise it, how do we decide?

And this really is a crisis complete with assembled relatives, last goodbyes, phone calls, absent and geographically distant friends, there are floods somewhere, the lover not answering her phone, the ambulance arriving and refusing to take her to die at a hospital other than RPA. I drive her, propped up on pillows in the back seat, wincing and screaming at every rut and bump, it is a slow journey at 2.00 am through the empty streets across the city, had it been raining? I can't remember, but it should have, and the city lights shining on the gleaming water.

Later we recount it all. Aghast. Drinking cognac. Relieved. Tears are always for yourself. They are not generous.

I go away. I come back to a different place.

I am painting the fence. A man comes from the local council with a survey. He askes me what I think is wrong with the community.

Last night, someone asked me, apropos of where I had bought the peas, 'Is he a wog?' This struck me as an unanswerable question. I ignored it. But I say to the man from the local council with his short-sleeved shirt and tie and clipboard, that what is wrong with the community is that it is gratuitously racist, that I can't believe the racism that goes on and on, as if it were a fact and not discredited, or a feeling that is not disgusting.

And, I say, Geoffrey Blainey makes it clear that it is not the absence of the intellectual cosmopolitan life here in the small country towns that is to blame. I suggest it is the silence, my own silence as well. Easy words thrown into conversation go unchallenged. We have been through it all so often before. It is easier. If I speak my mind there will be a family argument to spoil the homecoming dinner. Worse, they would come back with a few pat sentences and I would have failed again. But my safe silence is inexcusable. (And for me to come away and write it down for an audience that agrees with me seems like another sort of silence.)

It's all right in the city.

I come home early one summer morning after a night out. It is already hot. I have hitched from Rozelle to change clothes for work. I have left my keys on someone's bedroom floor. I have to break into my flat. The painter in the hallway assists me in a half-hearted and sceptical way. Finally I spring the lock with a piece of plastic. He refuses to be impressed. It's a relief to close the door. I run a bath and iron a shirt. I listen to the radio and am late for work. You can tell these days devoid of romance. They start calmer than most.

It is never simple or clear.
A great deal of talk goes round. We listen and talk, like a telephone. That distance. The machine.
We will make certain and uncertain decisions.
There's danger. The air crackles with distrust, horror, gossip, the ordinary. Loungerooms become. There's a party or two. There's a weekend. There's a point. We cannot sit about and talk, talk.
Sunday afternoon. Drinking wine at a meeting. I nod. Look around the room. Do not speak. I think this: be careful, do not speak.
There are waves of criticism. They come from a long way away. They are obscene.
We do not dance. They see us dancing anyway.
Meanwhile the embezzlers live high on Bellevue Hill. The money gone missing is too expensive to retrieve. A curious and specific inadequacy of a legal system that can do what it has expensively done to Lindy Chamberlain. Embezzlement's not good copy. Such a grey affair. A book on organised crime says, 'Look, don't be silly, it's not organised, it's just a few of the boys being boys.' It is favourably reviewed by a left-wing lawyer. Collaborators in simplicity. Companionable corruption. And (I can't resist this) lawyers, guns and money. Good lunch-time conversation. Nothing too serious, and never political or moralistic. There's a great deal more to be said.

Through all this there has been no moon.
The dangerous time.
The male ascendant.
The female principle absent.
But the dark side of the moon is still the moon.

Too much talk. At the famous literary pub I meet names that fit with poems and endure a woman who treats me like her dog. She pats me on the head. Lavish affection. She knows I am not a fool but she says she has 'discovered' women (this in 1986), as if we are a breed apart, or have only just arrived. Not *like* them. The embrace of difference. Something about the way we guess, I guess.

If she had been driving alone she would have sung all the songs she knew and she would have pulled into a motel and registered and fallen into a sleep with endless dreams and woken in the night to listen to the trucks on the highway and to remember nothing at all.
That would have been all right for one night.

They damage each other.
They are bruised with passion and desire.
They are vague and diligent. Robotic.
They are very busy.

I had heard shots in the night. I often heard shots in the night. What could have been. I open the paper in the morning and read about the man found shot dead in a Redfern street. It's nearby. I say, I thought I heard shots in the night. The man found dead in the nearby street was shot at three in the afternoon.

The cards are cool. Money is lost evenly for a while. Playing on. Pleasure in the game. The cards turn hot and you know you can't lose, up you go, aces and jacks, luxury luck, a taxi home whizzing fast down the Parramatta Road, lights and the rain, the street sparkling and reflecting, icon neon, appreciate the art ugliness of city scapes.

Post-modernism is such a first-world word.

We drove through the French countryside and past the nuclear power station. I didn't stop to take a photo. I thought about it. I'm not very good at taking photos. But I wish I had. It was brilliant. My first nuclear reactor. And it was so shiny and new and complicated and different to look at and there, just there, at the side of the road.

I go away. I come back to a different place.

Minimum requirements for a film about country life: one romantic weatherboard house, at sunset; one full moon; one windmill and tank (on tankstand); one sky full of stars (how difficult is it to film the sky filled with stars?); one haystack; one cluster of mail-boxes; one Holden ute; a couple of dirt tracks; the river, the bush.

I ring a friend in Sydney and arrange for somewhere to live.

The passionfruit cascade in the back yard. We harvest them each day and admire the way the vine becomes a curtain.
In the early morning the men who live in the cleared block two doors up light a big fire with their accumulated rubbish and stand around it drying their clothes and coats and blankets and mattresses after five days of rain.
The house that was there before them was supposed to be the oldest house in Redfern, the original farm house, once classified by the National Trust.
Some men slept over in the wreckage, to stop vandals and thieves, but someone got away with the fireplaces and someone else managed the water heater, the fittings, the windows, two good doors, the kitchen sink. The ancient camellia trees still stand and still bloom, and for a few months in winter the block is a good camping spot for the city's nomads.

Cigarettes matches ashtray. Climb the stairs as always the complete stranger and entirely at home.
The room. The changes and the same.
Not detection. *Mise en scene.* Books. The desk. Late at night.
Undress slowly. Fold the clothes or let them fall to the floor.
Cotton sheets.

It is very cold. Hold tight.
The wind blows through a broken window, another lover threw her shoe at it in anger. Hit and miss.
The line of desire from touch to breast to cunt.
Make love face to face to face.
Subject-object-abject-wanton. Wanting.
It makes no sense to analyse sex.
Love made, slightly reverent, very pagan.
Laugh and break apart, moved by all this.
Bodies have their own arguments and discussions.
They make dramatic scenes. Tears, melodramatics, haunted by ghosts, melancholy. It doesn't last long.
Fall back laughing and accusing, you, you, are fabulous, because any word will do, the adjectives of sex. (Love.)
In the morning go weak-kneed to work.
Secrets. Wanting more. The telephone.

It is evening, the early winter dark, sitting around the kitchen table, briefly:

The American says Sydney is like Paris was in the thirties.
The English woman says Sydney is so west coast, so LA. So unable to be taken seriously. Decadent.
I might say, yes, Australia is different, steal from my travelling friend who, finding the French with their nuclear tests in the Pacific, civil war in Kanaky, and Le Pen getting too many votes, (just ripe for the ironic); said yes, said:

Australia is different; it is a desert and there we eat sand.

NOTES AND ACKNOWLEDGEMENTS

FOR THEIR ASSISTANCE with the production of this book, we would like to thank: Bridget Bainbridge, Megan Bird, Ana Constantinou, Jane Crawley, Farrago, Jocey Ford, Anna Funder, Katrina Gas, Sabra Lazarus, Jenny Lee, Mathilde Lochert, Chris McAuliffe, Jenna Mead, Philip Mead, Peter Phipps, Michelle Proctor, Monica Raszewski, Alison Ravenscroft, Betty Rouch, Miranda Sandars, Shiralee Saul and Fiona Studdert. Special thanks to Mark Davis, Trish Luker and Lin Tobias.

We gratefully acknowledge the financial assistance of the Melbourne City Council.

JORDIE ALBISTON is thirty years old, a single mother of two, and a post-graduate student in Literature at LaTrobe University. She has been (seriously) writing poetry since 1987 and has had work published in *Hecate*, *Mattoid*, *Verandah*, *linQ*, and *Womanspeak*. She has read at venues including La Mama, Victoria College (Spoleto Fringe), the Montsalvat National Poetry Festival (1990, 1991) and various pubs. She was co-winner of the Wesley Michel Wright National Poetry Prize (1991).

BRIGITTE BARTA was born in Wellington, New Zealand, in 1965. When she was six months old her parents took her to live in Berlin, via Naples. Since then she has resided in different parts of Europe and England with long stretches of time spent in Melbourne in between. Currently she lives and works in Melbourne and is studying for a Graduate Diploma in editing and publishing.

MARY BASTABLE has lived for 39 years, 'did' fifteen of them in social/community work and social welfare administration, and finds she has two children. She is currently working on a Master's Degree in the area of women's life story texts. This piece is part of her practice of the politics of women's self-writing and is her first work to be published.

LISA MARIE BELLEAR (NOONUCCAL) lives in Melbourne where she works as a broadcaster on 3CR Community Radio's 'Not Another Koori Show' and on 3LO with Terry Laidler on Koori issues. She is founding member of the Ilbijerri Aboriginal and Torres Strait Islander Theatre Co-op Ltd. Lisa is also President of Koori Vision. 'Women's Liberation' was previously published in Hecate.

ANNETTE BLONSKI was born in Melbourne in 1951 to Eastern European parents. She is currently a research consultant to several film and arts organisations, and teaches screen studies at the Victorian College of the Arts, School of Film and Television. Much of her work has been informed by feminist and multicultural concerns. For many years, she wrote and published critical writing but has recently begun to work with fiction. An earlier version of 'Houses of Pleasure' was presented at the Cite Sight Site forum at Linden Gallery, St Kilda in 1991.

JOANNE BURNS is a Sydney writer. Her latest book is *on a clear day* (UQP Poetry 1992). 'album' is from a recently completed (but as yet unpublished) collection of futurist fictions and parables, *a stab in the dark*.

MARION CAMPBELL was born in Sydney in 1948. She has written two novels: *Lines of Flight* (Fremantle Arts Centre Press 1985) and *Not Being Miriam* (Fremantle Arts Centre Press 1988) and more recently has written for the theatre: *Dr Memory in the Dream Home* (in collaboration with composer, Noëlle Janaczewska). She teaches in the English and Comparative Literature Programme at Murdoch University. 'Once I was Fou Roux's Lover' and 'The Prowler' form part of a larger work in progress called 'On Being Cross-Eyed'.

CHRISTINE EDWARDS is 35 years old and was born in England. She started writing seriously about four years ago, and has had her short stories and poetry published in *Network*, *Studio*, *Oz Wide Tales,* and *Summer Readings in St Kilda 1991*. She also writes children's stories, poems, and picture texts, and has completed a novel for teenagers. She won the 1991 Mary Grant Bruce Award for a writer living in Gippsland. A mother of three children, she plans to return to part-time teaching this year.

EVELYN (ROBSON) was a Home Kid, Salvationist, single mother, communist, trainee traindriver.... Now a lesbian housing worker who performs and writes. She first performed 'Footplate Classics' in 1988 at a Radical Women fundraiser and adapted it for *Spot the Dyke*, Amazon Theatre, 1990. This is the first time her work has been published.

DIANE FAHEY is a poet who lives in Adelaide. She has published several collections of poetry including *Turning the Hourglass*. She has also been widely published in journals throughout Australia. 'Thirteen' appeared in *Memory* (a special issue of *Southerly*).

ANNA GIBBS teaches writing and textual theory at the University of Western Sydney, Nepean. She is co-editor of *Frictions* (Sybylla 1982) and *No Substitute* (Fremantle Arts Centre Press). Much of her current writing is done in the context of interdisciplinary arts collaborations. Parts of 'Terminal' have appeared in earlier versions in *Cultural History* and *Praxis M*, and have been produced for broadcast on ABC radio by *The Listening Room*.

SARA HARDY began her acting career in the 70s and, frustrated at the lack of good parts for women, began to write her own. Having devised many plays since then, Sara co-wrote *Radclyffe* with Adele Saleem and wrote *Vita! - A Fantasy*, which appears in *Heroines* (Penguin 1991). In 1991 Sara received a writer's fellowship from the Literature Board of the Australia Council. Her latest play is *Kindred Spirits*. Originally from England, Sara now lives in Melbourne.

JACKIE HUGGINS is an Aboriginal historian and writer from Queensland. She is a widely published author on Aboriginal women's business, with the majority of her work appearing in journals such as *Hecate*. She has completed a biography of her mother Rita, and is working on a collection of essays on history, racism and colonialism, as well as a collection of Aboriginal women's writings. Parts of 'Pretty Deadly Tidda Business' have previously appeared in *Hecate* and *Memory* (a special issue of *Southerly*).

NOELLE JANACZEWSKA is a NSW writer, director and visual artist. Writing mostly for live performance and radio, her work has been presented in Britain and Europe as well as throughout Australia. In 1991 she was awarded the NSW State Performing Arts Scholarship to undertake a period of study at the Institute of Theatre and Film in Hanoi. 'Still Waters Run Deep' is adapted from a performance work, *The History of Water*, developed with the assistance of a writer's grant from the Literature Board of the Australia Council.

MAYLN LAM was born in 1957. She is a teacher, presently working at Monash University, Gippsland, and writing a PhD on love stories.

RUBY LANGFORD 'GINIBI' was born on Box Ridge Aboriginal Mission in Coraki, on the north coast of NSW in 1934. She had a family of 9 children and raised them mostly by herself, working at fencing, burning off, ringbarking, pegging roo skins, and in clothing factories. Now 58, she has 21 grandchildren and is author of *Don't Take Your Love to Town* (Penguin 1988), and *Real Deadly* (Angus and Robertson 1992). She has also written the history of her people, the Bundjalung tribes, which will be published in 1993 as *My Bundjalung People*.

RAE LUCKIE (nee Kelly) was born in 1940 and raised by aunts in Orange and Parkes. Married to Barry for 31 years, they have three children. Rae has worked in a wide assortment of jobs with the NSW Police Department and in educational administration. She began a Masters in Communication in 1991. Her writing was nurtured by lecturer, Dr Anna Gibbs, Writer-in-Residence, Mary Fallon, and tutor, Jennifer Maiden. Accepted by TAFE as a full-time teacher of Communication, she has just completed a Graduate Diploma in Education at the University of Technology.

JAN MATTHEWS lives in Melbourne where she works as a shop assistant. After university she taught for a while at secondary level, and later completed a degree in theology. Having at last seen the error of her ways, she has 'put on purple', and now watches the world with some amusement/anger/curiosity from behind shop counters.

JAN McKEMMISH was born in Tongala, Victoria in 1950. She is the author of *A Gap in the Records* (Sybylla 1985), *Only Lawyers Dancing* (Collins Angus and Robertson 1992), and co-author with Pamela Brown of the play *As Much Trouble as Talking*, 1988. 'From Common Knowledge' was written when she was becoming interested in writing for performance, for the microphone. It is from the imminent novel *Common Knowledge* and has previously appeared in *Meanjin/Writers in the Park*, 1989.

TRISH McNAMARA lives in Sydney where she has studied writing at the University of Technology. She comes from a large family of cynics but still manages to dream.

PHILIPPA MOYLAN researched the novels of Edith Searle Grossmann in her MA thesis at the University of Auckland. She is currently pursuing further post-graduate studies on a part-time basis at the University of Melbourne and teaches a course on women's writing at the Institute of Education.

LUCY JEAN MROZIK has started writing since retiring as principal of a Melbourne High School in 1986. Her short stories have been published in several literary magazines and in an anthology, *Fictions '88* (ed. F Moorhouse).

Her writing has received several awards and commendations in competitions, and she has just completed her first novel.

ROSEMARY NISSEN describes herself as a writer/healer and teacher in both fields. Best known as a performance poet, she is a sometime editor, publisher, arts administrator, freelance fiction writer, journalist, and psychic artist. Now involved full time in Reiki, a method of natural healing. Has published *Universe Cat* (Pariah 1985) and *Small Poems of April* (Abalone 1991). Her writing has also appeared in various journals and anthologies.

VICKI PINGLE is an illustrator and writer. Currently working on a comic, and deserves tattoo equipment. She lives in Brisbane.

LILLIAN PREDIC-YOKSICH was born in Belgrade, Serbia, into an intellectual and artistic Serbian family. She has lived and worked in Melbourne since 1985, becoming an Australian citizen in 1989. Lillian has written poetry since she was five years old and has won numerous literary competitions. She also paints and has had several exhibitions. 'The Journey' was translated by Melanie Petranovic and is Lillian's first poem to be published in English.

MONICA RASZEWSKI was born in Melbourne of Polish parents. She works at the State Library of Victoria and as a freelance writer of fiction. She has written several short stories and is currently working on a novel. This is the first time her work has been published in a book.

GIG RYAN was born in Melbourne in 1956. She has published *The Division of Anger* (Transit Poetry 1982) and *Manners of an Astronaut* (Hale &Iremonger 1985). She has also been published widely in magazines. Gig is a poet, guitarist and singer.

TERESA SAVAGE was born in England in 1955 and now lives in Sydney. She has published children's stories, articles, previews, and short stories; her most recent work appears in the anthology *Bodylines* (Redress Press 1991). Teresa works as a mother and as a librarian; lives with her partner and their three children; is interested in reflecting working class origins and lesbian sexuality. Teresa is a member of the Sydney based Bluetongues Lesbian Writers Group.

ANGELA SEWARD lives in Bondi, NSW. She was born in Perth in 1958 and grew up in Peppermint Grove. She spent time in France in 1976. This is her first story published in a book. 'As Blind as a Blue Sky in Australia' has previously appeared in *Arm* 1991 and *Meanjin* 1992.

JYANNI STEFFENSEN is an Adelaide based artist, writer and critic. She is currently working on a PhD examining the construction of desire and sexuality in contemporary lesbian witing. She is a regular contributor to *Otis Rush, Photofile* and *Broadsheet*.

FRANCES STEPHANS is from Cornwall in England and currently lives in the Adelaide Hills. 'A Ghost in the Kitchen' is the first story she has written.

SUSAN LAURA SULLIVAN is a graduate of the Curtin University's creative writing course (Western Australia). She was born in Perth in 1967 but shifted to Melbourne in 1990. While in Perth, she co-edited Curtin University's creative writing magazine, *The Naked Eye,* and helped establish The Ridgey Didge Show, a creative writing programme on radio 6NR. She has performed numerous times in Perth and Melbourne and has had work published in *Northern Perspective, Going Down Swinging* and *Skirt*. She is currently working in Japan teaching English.

LINDA MARIE WALKER is a writer and artist living in Adelaide. Her illustrated book *Cherished Objects* (in collaboration with Paul Hewson) was published by the Experimental Art Foundation, Adelaide, in 1989. She has recently edited a collection of texts (and curated a touring exhibition) by Australian women on eroticism, titled . . . *but never by chance* . . . . The first section of 'Stationmaster' was published as 'Romance: the Station Master' in *Otis Rush* 5, February 1990.

SARAH WATERSON was born in 1963 and is a Sydney based visual artist. She is currently completing a master's degree in women's studies, in between her studio and tappings on Betty the computer.

DEBBIE WESTBURY was born 1954 in Wollongong NSW. Her poetry was first published in *Mother I'm Rooted* (1975, ed. Kate Jennings) and has been widely published since in literary journals and anthologies in Australia and overseas. Her first collection of poetry was *Mouth to Mouth* (Five Islands Press 1990) and a second collection, *Touching Ground,* is due out in 1993. She lives in Coledale, north of Wollongong, with her son, Luke, and makes a living out of sculpting, teaching and writing.

LINDA WESTE was born in 1963 and lives in Melbourne. She has had poetry published in various literary journals, including *Mattoid* and *Hecate*, and anthologised in *The Exploding Frangipani* and *Pink Ink*. 'Eins Zwei Drei' traces the history and integrity of a family of German-Australians since the 1930s.

It evolved from archival information and the writer's own interpretation of historical events, but began with the child questioning.

LAUREN WILLIAMS was born in 1958 in Melbourne. She discovered live poetry at various venues in 1983 and became involved thereafter. While sometimes referred to as a 'performance' poet, she prefers to avoid categorisations - 'poet' will do. Her collection 'Driven To Talk To Strangers', in the book *Live Sentences* (Penguin, 1991), was highly commended in the Anne Elder Award. She is currently associate editor with the literary anthology, *Going Down Swinging*.

ALSO FROM SYBYLLA PRESS

FICTION

Working Hot
MARY FALLON

In this award-winning novel, Mary Fallon's savage wit emerges with full force. She has created a raw and powerful representation of sexuality in women's lives.
  Kinky Trinkets, One Iota, Freda Peaches, Top Value, and ECR Saidthandone are women who traverse Fallon's landscape seeking love and evading the jumble of memory.

A Gap in the Records
JAN McKEMMISH

A Gap in the Records is a contemporary Australian novel in which a group of women control a world-wide spy ring. Through a juxtaposition of characters, time periods and writing styles, it pushes against stereotypes of women's writing. The result is an impelling look at the deliberate and accidental ways that power can be operated and resisted.

Quilt
FINOLA MOORHEAD

In this collection of Finola Moorhead's writing, short stories and poetry are finely stitched together by essays and reviews to produce new insights on the process of writing.
  Finola writes about women. She tells about their lives and speaks of women as writers, and of their relation to and experience of their craft.

Frictions: an anthology of fiction by women
EDITED BY ANNA GIBBS AND ALISON TILSON

This ground breaking anthology of Australian women's writing is a lively presentation of women's experience of life in Australia. The variety of content reflects the different cultural backgrounds, experiences and interests of the twenty-three contributors. The writing is daring and exploratory.

NON-FICTION

Between the Lines
BERNICE MORRIS

The course of Bernice Morris's life in the 1950s was shaped by events surrounding the Petrov affair. In this autobiography, she traces the extended impact on her family's personal life of some of the major political events of our time, in Australia and internationally. It has been claimed that no one was hurt by the Petrov affair. This book tells another story.

Taking the Revolution Home: work among women in the Communist Party of Australia: 1920-1945.
JOYCE STEVENS

In this illustrated volume, Joyce Stevens carefully documents the history of 'work among women' in the Communist Party in the inter-war and war years against a background of broader Australian politics of the period.
   Ten communist women who were active in this area of political life contribute their personal recollections of the issues, campaigns and ways in which their political commitment brought about changes in their own lives.